Text set in Times New Roman

Designed by Robert H. Brown

Cover art by Robert H. Brown

THE
TOYSHOP
AT THE END
OF THE WORLD

by
"Captain" Robert Brown

Illustrations by
Juan Pablo Valdecantos Anfuso

CONTENTS

PROLOGUE:
OUT OF TIME

Charlotte Cesare had waited for Calvin for five hours. Well, to be honest, Charlotte had waited for Calvin for five years, but it would be unfair for her to count that, as she sat at the little round table in the dark corner of the noisy pub where she worked.

Calvin had run into the pub in the early afternoon while she was wiping down tables and preparing for the evening's commotion. The twenty-five-year-old man, with messy, sandy blond hair and deep brown eyes was just six years older than she, and he had stammered out something about, "When I've tested my latest project it will finally be time! We will have all the time in the world to be together." He had smiled handsomely and slyly, in a way that implied he had a secret she could not guess.

But she was confident she guessed it. Charlotte was beautiful, and her parents had often said to her, "How long until that Calvin proposes? He's had years to make up his mind. I know you don't come from a family with money like he does, but if he's stuck around this long, surely he plans to propose."

So Charlotte waited patiently for Calvin to arrive, while Calvin fumbled about his attic apartment. This apartment was really more of a lab with a bed. It was cluttered and dark, with various worktables around the room containing different experiments. Vials of fluid, sealed orbs of varying sizes filled with pink gas, a device like a typewriter with a viewing screen on top, and a variety of unfinished toys all cluttered the room in a haphazard way.

Calvin was often cocky, but occasionally he was just excited. Today was one of those days. After a thousand tests of individual parts, and minor applications of his grandest theory, today he finally felt ready to test out the culmination of his plans.

In the center of the room was a cabinet the size of a wardrobe. There was a door in the center of the cabinet, and the outside of the box was wrapped in a labyrinth of copper pipe. The copper pipe connected eight glass orbs that were attached to the corners of the structure. They were filled with a pink gas. Unfortunately, many containers about the room also contained that same gas.

Calvin looked at the clock, "Dammit! I'm late to meet Charlotte." But then he chuckled. "Well, I suppose that will be irrelevant in a moment."

He stepped inside the cabinet. As he shut himself in, he whispered to himself, "The magical disappearing cabinet of Doctor Calgori," and he smiled. "What a fine adventure this will be. I'll nip out, and be back early to meet her, with an amazing story to tell."

And he thought of how patient and understanding Charlotte was with him.

Inside the cabinet it was dark, and he felt around for the throw switch. Well, here goes, he thought, and pulled the lever.

All at once the orbs at the corners of the cabinet glowed pink, the color of the sky just before a storm. This Calvin had expected, but unbeknownst to Calvin, all the other

orbs around the room were also beginning to glow.

Calvin's ears popped painfully. He had a sensation of sudden acceleration he did not expect. The cabinet started shaking, so much that he had to brace himself against the walls to remain standing.

Outside the cabinet, toys and half-made inventions were shaking and vibrating and dancing around the room, falling off tables and crashing to the floor.

The orbs all grew brighter, and there was a blinding flash, followed by a sucking sound.

If you had been watching from the street, staring up at the Victorian apartment building in the late afternoon, you would have seen the window grow brighter and brighter, until you saw a huge flash, heard a "crack!" and then saw the entire third floor of the building disappear completely! This severed two pigeons from the rooftop in half, and sent the others fearfully into flight.

The remaining top of the building shivered a bit, and then slowly crumbled in on itself.

A little more than two hundred years in the future, Calvin's cabinet reappeared. It reappeared three stories above the ground, and it ripped through the air at 100 miles per hour. This was not something Calvin anticipated when he designed the cabinet, and the result of it entering the air at this speed tore the wooden box instantly to pieces.

A large thick chunk of cabinet struck him on the head and knocked him unconscious.

Luckily, the air slowed his limp body considerably

before he hit the ground. It's the only reason he survived the collision.

Hours later he lay, eyes closed, face down in hot sand. His back was hot, his armpits and between his legs felt wet and sticky. He was dizzy.

Then he felt a kick in his side, and heard a voice. "Wake up. You're not dead." Then another kick. "I said, wake up!"

Calvin struggled to open his eyes. At first he saw nothing but the bright glow of a glaring yellow sky and white-hot sand. Then there were blurry shadows before him, and as they came into focus he saw grey and black uniforms. Around them, scattered in the sand, lay the contents of Calvin's apartment.

A pair of shiny black boots stepped into his view, and their owner squatted down in front of him. He was an angry-looking military officer, in small round sunglasses and wearing a uniform Calvin did not recognize. The officer held in his hand one of Calvin's 'thinking machine' experiments.

"Is this yours?" the officer asked, and it was more an accusation than a question. "Where did you get this?"

"Well," said Calvin, finding it hard to speak, but still managing to sound cocky. "I invented it!"

"That's what I thought!" said the officer with a frown. He stood, and motioned to his comrades. "To the Cage with him."

BELOW THE FLOOR

Chloe and Isabella sat in the dark at the top of a very old set of wooden stairs and listened. Inches above them

was the floor, but of course to them it was a ceiling and a door all at once. The line of the door glowed like a thin little smile, almost sinister, and it drew a stripe of light across their faces as they looked up at it. The two little girls, ages six and nine, had sat at the top of the stairs all evening, as they had done on many other evenings after their schoolwork and chores were finished.

The air was dead in their cramped apartment below the stairs. It was filled with the smell of dust and dankness, just as the apartment was filled with spiders, and broken furniture, and rotting wooden beams. They had not been outside for months, and their mother had not been fully awake for days, which they were getting used to, though it troubled them.

Their father had died before Isabella could remember. Chloe, being older, had a vague impression of a stern and angry man who often yelled at Mother, red in the face, until he coughed painfully into a handkerchief. The coughing would shake his entire body, until he would collapse exhausted into a chair, and say, "See what you do to me?"

One day he was no longer there to fight with Mother, and she became even more sad. That's when they moved into the apartment below the floor. Eventually Mother began coughing, too, and now Mother remained in bed, and slept, while the girls were left to manage for themselves.

Each day they cleaned, looked after their mother, and worked in their schoolbooks by the flickering amber light of dim bare glass bulbs. After all of this was done, they climbed to the top of the stairs, sat nearly silent in the dark, and listened. All day they heard footsteps and voices, and the voices were their entertainment.

There were child voices, some laughing, or crying. Some showing amazement, and some pretending a lack of amazement. Some pleading with parents, and some making demands of parents.

"Oh goodness me! She's the most beautiful thing I've ever seen!" a tiny girl's voice would say.

"Please, father, I'd do all the chores forever if I could have that tin soldier!" an excited boy would say.

"Last Christmas I got seventeen presents. They were all better than this crap. This one is so stupid, look, it can't even get into the castle! And look how easily its head breaks off! Mother, buy me that castle!" a horrible child would say.

There were also adult voices, some disciplining mostly good children, and some folding to the whims of very bad children. Some adults were playing with their kids, and this was most pleasing of all to hear. Those parents were as full of amazement as the children themselves.

The two little girls would sit all afternoon and evening, after their chores and schoolwork were finished, and listen to the voices; trying to imagine the amazing toys.

Chloe and Isabella had never gone past the trapdoor at the top of their stairs. Their Uncle James, who was a very nice man, had said it was better for the girls not go into the shop, as they "might be seen." The fear of being seen had not been explained to the girls, although it had been imparted to them. James was so kind, and loving, and smart, that they had never thought to disobey him, though the temptation had been very, very strong.

It was now late in the evening, and the voices had

stopped half an hour ago. The girls now whispered about the voices, trying to guess what the kids looked like.

"I'll bet that small girl with the little animals had beautiful blond ringlets, a white lacy hat, and a happy face," Chloe said dreamily.

"I think she had big brown eyes, and short brown hair like mine. I liked her, she seemed nice," said Isabella.

"I wish we could play with her," said Chloe.

"I'll bet that mean boy was ugly, with freckles," Isabella said.

"I have freckles!" Chloe objected.

"You have pretty freckles and pretty long red hair. I'll bet he had fat red cheeks and ugly freckles."

"Humph," Chloe said.

They were getting hungry. No dinner had yet come, though they had expected it hours ago. This had happened before, so the girls had given up on the prospect. It was Uncle James who brought dinner, and in his absence Chloe became worried.

Little Isabella didn't blame James for not bringing dinner. She did, however, view lack of dinner as an injustice, and this injustice seemed like a justification to her.

So she said, "I want to see the toys."

"We can't go up!"

"Yes we can, look, you just push here and it opens!" And Bella reached out to push.

"Bella!" Chloe exclaimed, pulling Isabella's hands

down from the trapdoor. "We shouldn't go up! We might be seen."

"The shop's closed now. Look, there's hardly any light coming from above, and it's been ages since we heard a voice."

"I don't think we should."

"Don't you want to know what they look like?" Bella said, meaning the toys.

"Of course I do, but James said we shouldn't."

Bella tried to see Chloe's face in the darkness, but could only see a thin orange stripe where light from the trapdoor traced Chloe's round cheeks and small nose.

"But there is no dinner tonight, and my tummy hurts," said Isabella, and she frowned in the dark, dusty stairwell.

"Mine too," said Chloe, and she frowned as well.

This argument was working. Logically, it didn't make sense. Toys and food had nothing to do with each other. But on another level, Chloe could see that not getting dinner again was unfair, and it felt like fate in some way owed them this. They had hungered to see the toys longer than they had hungered for food, and it seemed at least one of these hungers could be satiated.

So Chloe said, "Maybe we can just push open the trap, and look from here. Besides, it'll take your mind off your tummy hurting."

So slowly, Chloe and Isabella pushed open the trapdoor, and with trepidation, they stepped out into the Toy Shop.

INTO THE TOY SHOP

The floor of the Toy Shop was of dark wood so polished that it looked like pooled water. Reflected in this dark water were dozens of ornately carved and richly painted cabinets, waist high to an adult but chest high to a child.

On these cabinets sat the toys. In the unlit shop, the girls could only gain the vaguest impression of the toys, but what they could see seemed marvelous. Upon each cabinet sat a miniature world, silhouetted in the darkness. Castles around which airships flew in silent battle. Victorian manors being visited by horse and carriage. Battlefields filled with battalions of soldiers, and still and silent machines of war. All sat silent in the dark.

Immediately in front of them was a toy circus. As they approached the circus, it lit up. Tiny lanterns on tiny poles and miniature strings of amber light flickered and sparkled. A large and colorful tent the size of a coffee table was displayed in the warm glow, surrounded by little gypsy vardos attached to elephants. The elephants were made of segmented pewter, and they were mechanical, so they lumbered slowly and gracefully as a real elephant would. Each elephant was the size of an adult's hand, and they were being led by little mechanical circus men and women.

The girls gasped in awe, eyes sparkling in the circus' light.

As they walked closer to the toy, the big top parted and swung open, revealing three rings, surrounded by bleachers filled with miniature people. Little mechanical horses began to run around the center ring while, inches above, a pair of aerialists swung and leapt between trapezes. A tiny organist in the corner played a miniature calliope, and the music varied from silly to dramatic, depending on what act was being performed in the rings.

Next to the circus tent was a hat of black silk, with a tall flat top, made to fit a child. Isabella picked it up and put in on. Immediately the horses stopped running, the aerialists halted, and three little clowns walked slowly to the center of the middle ring and stood still, looking up at Isabella.

"Oh, don't stop!" she said, thinking she said it in vain.

"Command us," said the middle clown, who was tall and slender and had a friendly but goofy smile. "You are the Ringmaster."

At this unexpected reply, Chloe gave a little gasp and covered her mouth, while Isabella was so shocked she stumbled backward into something behind her which knocked the hat off her head.

She pulled herself to her knees, and picked up the hat. She turned to see what she had bumped into. It was another cabinet, and on this cabinet stood a little silver knight in gleaming armor, with sword and shield. He was just ten inches tall, and towering over him was a huge dragon, the size of a large dog, with scales of alternating copper and brass. One claw held a delicate princess in a dress of pale blue silk, who now squirmed, and kicked, and beat at the dragon with tiny fists, trying in vain to free herself from the serpent's copper grip.

As Isabella watched, the dragon inhaled and belched forth a shower of sparks at the knight, who dropped to his knees and hid valiantly behind his shield. The sparks glanced off the knight's shield, and many sprayed past and hit Isabella harmlessly.

But then the dragon and the knight were still.

After a moment, Chloe said, "Why did they stop? Did you break it?"

"No, milady," said the knight. "You need to tell us what happens next." And he waited, looking at the two girls from behind his tiny shield.

Again the girls were stunned, but this time they were a little more ready for toys that talked back.

"How?" asked Chloe.

"Narrate the story, milady" said the knight.

"Oh!" exclaimed Chloe. "Um." She paused to put on an official storytelling voice. "The brave and handsome knight pulled out his sword..." As she said this, the small knight lifted his sword above his head. "...And ran at the Dragon." The knight lifted his shield above his head like an umbrella, and ran at the dragon.

"Hah-hah!" The girls clapped.

"But the Dragon grabbed the knight," said Isabella, and the glittering beast reached out a huge talon, and snatched the knight, glaring at him with rage-filled eyes.

"Then, the knight stabbed the dragon," said Chloe, and the little animated suit of armor thrust its sword against the dragon's claw. The dragon released him at once and pulled back, sucking his cut hand while holding the princess to its chest like a teddy bear.

The two girls laughed delightedly.

"Tell the knight to run up his back!" said a tiny voice behind them. The three clowns, and two of the aerialists from the circus stood watching.

There was a distant screeching noise, and the toys all looked towards the front on the shop in fear, then struck poses and were still. This was the first time the girls had looked towards the front of the shop, and through the large plate glass they could see a black and foggy street. The shadows of two men were dragging a third immense body towards the door of the shop, and laboring hard to do so.

Chloe and Isabella ducked just behind a cabinet, and peeked between the now-still dragon's legs. They watched the two men prop the third against the glass, and the older of the two shadows fumbled in his coat pocket to produce a set of keys.

A fourth figure in the street now walked sternly up to the three at the door. This new figure stood very straight, and pointed at the limp giant with a baton. The shadow with the keys then argued with the man with the baton, pointing at something above the shop window.

"We should go back," Chloe whispered to Isabella, and she glanced around for the trapdoor.

"Who's that giant on the ground?" Isabella asked.

"We should go back before we are seen. We shouldn't be seen!" Chloe said, and she grabbed Isabella's arm and pulled her towards the basement door.

There was a sharp snap as the shop door unlocked, and Bella lifted the trap door in the floor and slipped in. Chloe then backed into the stairway herself, and the last thing she saw as she lowered the door shut was a tiny knight at the edge of a cabinet giving a small wave goodbye to her.

THINGS THAT ARE NOT FAIR

Late into the night the girls flipped and turned in their rag beds in the basement. Chloe's bed was made of what had once been old couch cushions but now showed as much stuffing as upholstery. Bella's "top bunk" was a striped green and white sheet tied between rafters, hammock style, above Chloe's bed. And the two girls tossed and turned in their beds all night long. They had been so excited by their first view of the fabulous toys that there was no sleeping.

"That princess was so beautiful!" Chloe exclaimed in a whisper.

"She was brave. She never stopped fighting. Next time we should let the princess wear the armor and sword," said Isabella.

"I don't think the knight could take the armor off. I'm not sure that knight was made of anything more than armor. He might just be empty inside."

"Still, the princess should have a sword."

"Do you think you can play with the circus and the knight at the same time? It would be fun to have the knight ride an elephant to fight the dragon."

"The elephant was too small, it would have looked like the knight was riding a baby elephant to war."

"Ha-ha! That would still be wonderful!"

Their talk went on like this for hours. Eventually they fell asleep.

When Bella woke, Chloe was not in her bed. She

climbed out of her "top bunk" and onto Chloe's bed, then onto the much-swept-though-never-clean black brick floor. She crept by memory to the exposed wall switch, and flicked on the single bulb that dangled in the center of the room. Through a doorway she saw the bed of her mother. Her mother's hand was clutching a tissue spotted with red. Through another doorway she saw the kitchen, with wood stove and sink, and a stack of dishes they had washed the night before.

On the counter in the kitchen was a familiar brown paper bag. Uncle James brought food while we slept! Bella thought and, remembering she had not eaten the night before, she ran to the kitchen. She pulled out a hard dry loaf of bread, several cans of baked beans, a stick of butter, six eggs, a mostly unspoiled onion, and a bottle of pills.

Isabella emptied out the bag, wadded it up and put it in the stove. She then pulled several lumps of coal out of a tin bucket, and put them on top of the paper. She took matches, and lit the paper, and while it sputtered and attempted to light the coal, she put butter in a rusty cast iron pan, and put the pan on the stove. She then skipped out of the room, through the main room, and into a closet that had a dirt wall. Growing in the dirt were dozens of fat, dull white mushrooms. She picked four the size of her hand and sprinted back to the kitchen. Here she cut the mushrooms in quarters with a dull knife, and dropped them into the sizzling butter. She then took a slice off the onion, diced it, and dropped it into the butter, along with three eggs. She stirred the mix until the eggs turned opaque and fluffy, then grabbed the pan with a rag, and scraped some of the omelet onto a tin plate.

She took the plate and a fork, and the bottle of pills, and a glass of nearly clean water into her mother's room. She now had the task of waking her mother long enough to get her to take the pills, and eat some of the omelet, before her mother fell back asleep. Later she would help her mother to the bathroom. It was a heart-wrenching ritual, and each day mother would stay awake a little less, and eat a little less, and Isabella would try to smile and only cry a little afterward while cleaning up.

Isabella was six.

Isabella then took the cast iron pan and remaining omelet, and two forks, and headed to the top of the stairs. In the dark she couldn't see her, but Isabella was right to guess that Chloe was sitting there, trying to peer through the crack into the toy store.

There was a jingle of the front doorbell, and though Bella was silent, Chloe said, "Sssh! Here come the children!"

It was Saturday, so the girls were giving themselves the day off school. They sat all day listening to the children play. It was even more rewarding now, because they knew the toys near the trapdoor, and could imagine the games that were being played.

"The elephants will now do a dance!" said a boy, doing his best ringmaster voice. The girls imagined the elephants dancing, and when the boy and his sister laughed, Chloe and Isabella laughed with them.

"Oh, Mother, I would do anything to have that tin knight!" said another boy, and the girls made nervous little fists and held their breath, for fear their new friend would be sold before they had a chance to play with him again.

"Oh, I don't think that's tin, Billy. That looks like...oh my, silver! Billy, I don't think Mommy could afford that!" The girls exhaled and relaxed their grip.

The girls sat at the top of the stairs in the darkness, and at the end of the day when the shop went quiet, and the light in the crack of the door went dim, they pushed out again. There was no discussion this time, this was now a thing they did.

Again they saw the shiny dark wood floor, and the polished cabinets, and they saw the silhouettes of cities and castles and dragons and airships poised in the darkness.

Chloe went straight to the circus, and snatched up an elephant, carefully detaching it from its vardo. As she turned, she saw the knight sitting headless and defeated, in front of a sympathetic- looking dragon. On Isabella's shoulder sat the princess, with sword, shield, and helmet, and Bella said, "Let's take them somewhere to play."

They passed a table where two foot-long pirate ships exchanged fire in a sea of slow-motion waves. They passed a massive field in miniature, where soldiers the size of thimbles now basked in the grass, enjoying a much needed rest to their battle. They passed a red stone desert canyons, above which balloons and Zeppelins and bi-planes and triplanes swirled endlessly around like fish in an aquarium.

They came to a cabinet containing nothing but a wicker basket full of something that resembled ornate tea trays.

"I wonder what these do," said Chloe, gently setting down the miniature elephant. She pulled out one of the trays, and saw that it was a tiny wall, ten inches tall and twelve inches wide. It contained wainscoting, wallpaper, a multi-paned glass window complete with curtains, two wall sconces, and a tiny wall switch. She flicked the switch with her fingernail, and the lights came on.

"Oh, how pretty!"

"I see whatcha do!" Bella said, and she began pulling the walls out of the basket. Each wall magnetically linked to other walls at the corners, and within minutes they had created a vast and sprawling Victorian manor, complete with running water, working stoves, electric lights, and a slide down the grand entry's main stair. The tiny princess watched the whole construction process, helmet in lap, while sitting atop the tummy of the sleeping elephant. As she watched, the princess clapped with joy. The house was exactly her size.

Once the elephant and the princess had moved in, leaving the elephant in the front yard to serve as a watchdog, they carried the headless knight over, along with several of the clowns. The knight stomped up to the princess, snatched back his helmet, and mumbled, "How'd you like me to wear your head?"

The girls, leaving the toys to live in their new home, wandered deeper into the toy store.

In the farthest back wall was a door marked Workshop. The thought that this was the origin of all these amazements felt magical, and to visit such a place seemed mischievous.

They opened the frosted glass door, and peeked in. This room was not as pretty as the toyshop's main room. It had unpolished stone floors, and lining every bare wooden wall

THE TOY SHOP AT THE END OF THE WORLD

were a thousand hand tools, hung in rows of descending size.

In the center of the workshop was a table, and on the table lay a massive figure, a shadow mountain, prone in a pile of broken toys.

"Is that the man they carried in last night?"

"I'm not sure. Maybe..." replied Chloe, but she was interrupted by the toyshop's front doorbell. The two little girls climbed under the worktable and hid.

The two men they had seen the night before had walked into the shop, and they were talking in hushed voices. Chloe recognized the voice of Uncle James, a kind-hearted young man in his early thirties, with brown unruly hair, and ice-blue eyes.

"I understand they can't stay here forever, Calvin, but where are they to go? Their mother is sick, and cannot work for them. They have no father, and so there is no income to pay the taxes for their 'consumption points,'" James implored.

"James," replied the older man in sympathetic but condescending tones. "You are–passionately–misunderstanding me, as you always do. I am not saying they can't remain living in my basement, I'm saying they shouldn't. That is no life for a child, and it's probably aggravating their mother's sickness. Don't let your passion make decisions for you, it will typically make the wrong ones."

This was the voice of Calvin Calgori, the toy master. If he often was condescending, he had a right to be. Calvin, though in his fifties, had the energy and curiosity of a

27

ten-year-old, coupled with a knowledge of chemistry and clockworks and physics beyond anybody still alive. He had spent the last twenty-five years in the forcible employment of the government, creating things he would rather forget, and as a reward for his service he had been allowed to retire and open a toy shop which he named "Herr Drosselmeyer's Toys" (after the character in the Nutcracker Ballet).

"But Cal," James went on. "There aren't any other options. Nobody knows the laws better than myself. If a family cannot earn enough consumption points, the family members are 'relocated.' My sister and her children have no income, and if discovered they will be split up and placed into families that don't want them, to be another burden on their financial obligations."

"Is that what you think 'relocating' means? That the children will simply be moved to other families? I wish that was what I thought it meant," Calgori said darkly. "I see your point, but all the same, we need another plan. If the current system doesn't work for them, we need to step outside that system."

"Cal, you know what that kind of talk leads to. You're implying life outside the city, which we all know isn't allowed…" James was interrupted by a motion on the main worktable. "How is this one? Does he have some parts worth salvaging?"

"Well," Calgori said, walking around the table, "…his gyros and rods are bent, so he can't walk. He can't keep his balance. But I should be able to straighten them out. It might make more sense to fix him than scrap him."

"But can you repair his mind? He attacked a bunch of his fellow prison guards with his branding iron. They say he showed signs of too much awareness. He was not following orders, and he was making decisions for himself. Typically in the Tower we just scrap the machines that show signs of that kind of thing."

"Aw, James, don't be a fool like the rest of them. They complained for twenty years that my automatons were dimwitted. Honestly, I think they were just using them as scapegoats for their own mistakes. So I upgraded my automatons to be at least as intelligent as their masters, and now their masters outlaw the intelligent ones. They feel threatened."

"Only if they are too intelligent, Calvin. They are supposed to be machines. Laborers. If they think independently, how can they work as part of a team? Once they appear to think like people, they become people in the minds of those watching. And then it looks like slavery."

"Everything about the city is slavery."

"Doctor Calgori! Please, don't put me in the position of having to report you. Please don't talk like that around me." James was looking worried, and he tried to get back on topic. "But you're saying this one is broken?"

"Knowing right from wrong is not 'broken.'"

"Right and wrong is subjective, Cal. If your machine doesn't have the same definition of right and wrong as our government, then it's broken. And dangerous."

"James, you're a good man, but a stupid one." Calgori sighed, and set his pliers on the workbench. "Forgive me, I'm tired. I will see you tomorrow night. Leave an old man to rest?"

James sighed, and looked with pity at Calgori, who

did indeed look old and tired. James would get no more conversation from Calgori tonight, so he turned in frustration and left the shop.

The second he was gone, Calgori straightened up again, and paced around the room collecting various tools from the walls. He placed calipers, pliers, screwdrivers with bizarrely shaped tips, and tools too specific and varied to be described in a tin bucket, and took them to the table in the center of the room.

Calgori then began unscrewing metal plates from the sleeping giant's chest. As he did so, the girls heard a low, sad, scraping metallic voice, "I can't move, Father. Why can't I move?"

This voice sent a shiver down Chloe and Isabella's little spines. It was so sad, so defeated.

"Don't be afraid. You fell a very long way, and much of your insides have been crushed. But if I can make you, I can fix you."

"Was I wrong?" The quiet but ominously low voice vibrated the toys on the table around him.

"Wrong about what?"

"Was I wrong to defend that lady? She was scared. They were hurting all those people, and she was scared. I was supposed to hurt her, too, but I did not know why, so I wouldn't. And so the other automatons pulled her from my arms, and pushed me from the Tower's top."

"No, you were not wrong. They were wrong. You did the right thing, but sometimes doing the right thing hurts more than doing the wrong thing."

"That doesn't seem…right," said the brass man.

"Well, it's not 'fair', if that's what you mean. But that's why it was right. The world does not come equipped with a mechanism for fairness built into it. That's what good people are for. To put the fairness into the world."

"But I am not people," said the brass man, in a voice that sounded like it was a painful thing to say.

"Yes, you are. They may not want you to be, but you are. You are better 'people' than they are."

Sitting under the table now, the little girls, who barely understood this talk, could sense they had something deeply in common with the brass giant on the table. Something was not fair to all three of them. Something so very not fair, that none of them were supposed to exist at all.

Bella and Chloe continued to hide under the table, while the toy maker fixed and talked with the mechanical giant.

The hardest part of being a small child hiding is that you get bored and when a child gets bored, she starts to play with just about anything around. It's instinct, and it's uncontrollable. Bella could see some of the broken toys hanging over the edge of the table under which they hid, and couldn't help herself. So, slowly and quietly, she reached her tiny pink fingers up to the side of the table to grab a tiny doll.

But before she could grasp it, the tips of her fingers touched it, and it rolled just out of reach. She frowned, but before she could be sad, the doll slid back into view.

The giant had pushed it back to her!

She took it, but was now too nervous to play with it. The giant must know we are here, she thought, and she looked at Chloe with guilt. Chloe only put her finger to her lips, her eyes wide with panic. They did not understand why they hid below the floors of the toyshop, only that they were not to be seen. They had some warning that the consequences would be dire, but they did not know who they were hiding from. Perhaps the brass man, perhaps the toymaker.

"Well, that's all I can do tonight, my large friend. I'll be back in the morning, and see if we can get more of your insides straightened out. Still, you should be able to move now."

"Thank you."

"You're welcome," said Calgori. "Good night." And the doctor left the room by the spinal iron staircase in the corner, turning out the light as he left, and locking the door at the top of his stairs behind him.

The room was dark. All the girls could hear was the sound of the giant, the mechanisms in his exposed chest whirring quietly.

Finally, it spoke in a grinding, rattling voice. "Why do you hide?"

Chloe said, "We are supposed to hide." Then, after a pause, "Why didn't you tell on us?"

"Because I did not know why you hid."

"Are you going to tell on us?"

"No. Not if you were doing what you were told to do." He paused, then went on, "A person should not be in trouble for doing what they believe to be the right thing."

The girls were silent. They agreed with this, but felt they didn't quite understand all that was being said.

"Can we go?" asked Chloe.

"Why would you ask my permission?" said the machine.

"Because you are a grownup," said Chloe.

"Have you never met an automaton before?" asked the machine.

"No."

"Well, we don't tell living people what to do. They tell us what to do."

"But we are kids. Kids don't tell grownups what to do. They ask what they are allowed to do," Isabella said. "Have you never met a child before?"

"No. I have not." This was not exactly true, but the giant wished it was true, and all were silent.

Then the machine added, "I am unaware of the protocol for automatons and children. Not here in this setting." He sounded worried. "Perhaps we should keep this a secret until I find out what the rules are. Otherwise one or all of us might get into trouble."

ABOVE THE ROOF

The next morning it was Chloe's turn to make breakfast, and so Bella slept a little longer in her hammock in the rafters above Chloe's bed. Her view at this height would have been dirty under-floor and moldering wood, if not for the countless drawings made by her and Chloe. The drawings covered the ceiling, and the walls, and the rafters, and each drawing was a window into a world they would rather live in than their own; with trees, sunshine, animals, and smiling families.

They took their breakfast at the top of the stairs, listening to what they could now recognize as children directing the circus, or children directing a battle between and the knight and the dragon.

One little boy said, "Where is da princess? Dat dragon used to hold a princess, and now she's not dare!" Chloe and Isabella giggled.

"That's because she lives in a proper mansion now!" Chloe said to Bella in whisper.

When the shop had finally closed, the girls crept up and out of the basement hatch. This time instead of playing with toys, they crept into the workshop.

The brass giant now sat straddling the work table, as you or I might straddle a bench, hunched over a bit to keep his head from hitting the dangling electric light bulbs.

"You're looking much better today, Gyrod," Chloe said.

"Gy– rod." The machine ground the syllables a bit as he

said them.

"Isn't that your name?" Chloe asked. Bella crawled up onto the worktable between the giant's knees. She pulled out a mechanical winged horse that had somehow found its way into her possession on the short trip from the stairs to the workshop.

"I don't know if it's my name. No one has ever called me by a name," he replied.

"But I thought I heard the toymaker call you by that name," Chloe said.

"Father did?" Gyrod looked surprised and pleased, in the same way you might be surprised to find an extra one hundred dollar bill in your previously empty pocket.

Isabella grabbed one of Gyrod's huge hands, and pressed and pulled the fingers until it was the shape of a man, and placed it on the horse. Gyrod gently allowed it, and Isabella trotted the horse and the hand-man around the table.

"What is this?" said Gyrod, meaning the winged horse.

"It's a Unisus," said Bella matter-of-factly.

"A Unisus? I don't think I know what that is."

"It's a unicorn with wings," Bella said, looking up into the giant's face.

"A horse with a horn and wings. Unicorn and Pegasus together. Unisus," said Chloe, who had invented the word. She grabbed some broken doll furniture from off another table, and started to arrange a small home for the Unisus.

"Your Unisus needs winding," said Gyrod, looking sadly at the motionless toy.

35

"Gyrod, where are you from?"

"Not here," Gyrod said. "I was made in another workshop of Father's. In the Tower. That's where I worked before I was let go."

"What does 'let go' mean?" asked Chloe, although she thought she might guess what it meant. She vaguely remembered her father being 'let go' from his work, before Bella was born. This was why they had to move into the basement, although she didn't understand how those two events could be related.

"Perhaps 'let go' is the wrong word. I was holding on, and they made me let go, and I fell." Gyrod pointed with his non-horse-riding hand to huge dents and scrapes down one side of his arm and legs.

"That's horrible! Why would they do that?" exclaimed Chloe, looking angry and sympathetic at the same time.

"Because I didn't do what I was told."

"You were being bad?" Chloe and Bella now had stopped playing and were both staring sympathetically up into the giant's glassy eyes.

"No. I was being good. For once."

"That doesn't make sense. Why would you get punished for being good for the first time? Shouldn't you have gotten punished all the times you were bad?" asked Bella.

Gyrod's glowing glass eyes were changing color from green to a sort of orangish color. The giant's face could make no expressions, but its reddening eyes looked angry. Chloe nervously took a step farther away from Gyrod, and looked around the room at the size of the space under the tool cabinets that lined the walls.

But Bella went on, "Maybe it's because you weren't being a good listener. What were you supposed to do?"

Gyrod was silent.

Then he said, "I can show you, if you'd like."

"That's okay! I think we need to go..." said Chloe, backing towards a hiding space under a cabinet.

"Yes, please!" said Isabella, who was not seeing the change in Gyrod's eyes. "Please show us!"

Isabella had the feeling this somehow meant an adventure, and she was not wrong. The giant scooped Bella up in his arms, and stood. He un-straddled the work table, and in one stride crossed the workshop, then climbed up the iron spiral staircase in the corner. He was really too big for this staircase, and as he climbed it he reminded Chloe of a spider squeezing out of a hole too small for its body.

Chloe had no choice now but to follow. The brass giant had Isabella.

The stairs opened into a dark luxurious apartment, obviously the toymaker's. The toymaker must have gone to dinner, as the apartment was empty, save for its threadbare silken sofas and deeply scratched leather wingback chairs, covered in books of science or half-made toys.

On the far side of the apartment was a large iron door, covered in rivets and locks. The giant held Isabella with one arm, while he agilely unlatched each lock with his other hand. He then slid the iron door to one side, and stepped out into a dreary hallway lined with peeling grey-on-grey striped wallpaper.

The hall was at least tall, so that Gyrod could stand up properly. This meant his stride was now nearly five times Chloe's, so Chloe had to jog to keep up with him.

She wanted to say, "Please don't show us how you were once bad! Please just tell us, and then let us go back to our basement!" but she was now too afraid to say anything. Was this what they had been hiding from? She thought briefly about trying to kick the machine in the legs, to get it to drop Isabella, but Chloe couldn't imagine that kicking iron and brass pipes would do anything but hurt her and leave the giant unfazed.

Bella sat calmly cradled in the machine's arm.

Halfway down the hall they came to a small elevator with a painted wrought-iron door. The doorway was perhaps half the width of the giant's shoulders, and he sighed when he saw this. Then he turned to continue down the hall.

At the end of the hall was a stairwell. Gyrod looked up, and saw the square spiral of flights of stairs ascending twenty floors above them. He then looked at the small stairs, built for the stride of a man, not a giant, and again he sighed.

Then, most unexpectedly, he pulled Isabella up to his mouth, opened his jaw, and bit down on the back of her overalls. As she dangled from his mouth, Gyrod snatched Chloe and tucked her under one arm. Chloe screamed, but the machine was didn't seem to notice..

He put a huge foot on the cast-iron handrail, and stretched his other arm to the base of the stairs one flight above. And so by pulling, dangling, standing and stretching, he climbed all twenty floors up the center of the stairwell, completely skipping the stairs altogether.

Chloe was in a panic. She had become accustomed to small enclosed places. She found them cozy, like a mouse finds a toilet paper tube cozy. Dangling twenty floors above a stairwell was horrifying, and it made her freckled face red and her eyes fill with tears. One tear rolled off her cheek, and fell past the giant's huge steel feet, and down six floors before hitting the dusty concrete below.

Isabella was just waiting to see whatever the giant had to show her.

The very top of the stairwell ended at an old wooden door. The door was locked, but the giant pushed with his spare hand, slowly increasing pressure until the hinge of the door bent, pulling its screws from the wall. The door popped open then, and fell off into blackness.

There was now wind blowing in the door, and outside they could see stars, both above and below them.

The giant stepped out.

They were on the precarious rooftop of an elaborately ornamented Victorian skyscraper. Behind them, the roof continued up like a pyramid, until it peaked in an iron spire. Before them the edge of the roof was regularly spotted with large ugly gargoyles–mouths open, eyes glaring, and tongues rolling to the side.

There were stars in the windy black sky, and the twinkling lights of buildings all around below them.

Gyrod looked left, then right, and then said, "It must be on the other side." He turned, and walked along the edge of the building, placing his free hand on the heads of the

gargoyles to steady himself, with Chloe tucked under one arm, and Isabella dangling from his mouth.

There were buildings all around them, huge, like the one they stood on. They were ornate Victorian or Art Nouveau in design, but coal blackened and filthy. At the top of many were weathervanes swinging nervously in the wind, or large kites, black in the dark of the night.

This was the first time the girls had been to a rooftop, and indeed the first time they had been outside in a very long time. As her eyes got used to the darkness, Chloe could see that each city block was contained within a huge wall. The city itself, though vast, was enclosed in the largest wall yet, and past that wall was nothing but blackness. As she watched, the fierce wind tore one of the large kites free of its mooring. The wind carried it up, away from the building tops, and finally over the farthest wall and out into the blackness beyond the city.

Then Chloe looked up at the stars, and thought she saw figures, like specters, even blacker than the night sky, drifting far above her. Seeing them made her feel cold. Something deep in the back of her mind, the part children reserve for primal fears unexplained, told her that these specters were why she and Isabella lived in the basement. When Uncle James said, "Don't be seen," it was these specters he was talking about. She suddenly no longer feared Gyrod.

The giant rounded a corner, and stopped.

"There," he said, and he stretched one arm out to point.

Ahead of them, blocking out both city lights and stars, was a tower. The Tower. It was so tall that three-quarters of the way up, it disappeared into a misty shroud of clouds, only to stab out again above them and continue on up. The top of the tower was ringed in spires, and the spires reminded Chloe of the crown of an evil king she had seen in a very old book. The specters were coming and going from this tower's top, each one dropping a small shadow into the crown, then whirling and flying off into the darkness.

There were few windows in the tower, and even fewer lights. Where the lights were on, the girls saw bars blocking the windows.

Chloe thought, Why would they need bars? Nobody would try to get into a place so horrible as that. Maybe people trying to get out? Surely they'd die if they jumped from such a height. And briefly it occurred to her that maybe what was inside the tower was so horrible that jumping from the window would be preferable to staying inside. She shivered.

"That is where I am from," Gyrod said, and he set Chloe and Isabella between two gargoyles before folding his massive legs and sitting down himself.

"I worked at the very top. If you work there, you call it 'The Tower'. If you are brought there, you call it 'The Cage'." He paused. "I have also heard it called the Change Cage. I do not know why."

"What are those shadow-bugs bringing to the top of the Cage?" Isabella asked, with no fear in her voice. She was pointing at the specters, which could now be seen more clearly as skeletal figures hanging from a bloated bug-like armored body.

"Progressors."

"What is a pro guesser?" Isabella asked.

"I'm not sure. That's just what they call them. It has something to do with the walls, and laws," Gyrod said, puzzled.

"What are laws?" asked Isabella.

"Well, the city has rules called 'laws'. Laws tell you what to do, so that the city can run perfectly, and stay exactly how it is, without changing. If you ignore these laws, and do something different, you might change the city. It's the job of the police to keep the city from changing."

"But maybe the city should be changed. It's not very pretty… or happy… or nice," said Chloe, looking into the darkness below her and smelling the foul, grease-ashy air. She could hear someone crying in an apartment below.

"Well, if you tried to change it, a policeman would stop you. He would pull you out into the street, and a harpy," and here Gyrod pointed towards the specters going to and from the Tower's rooftop, "would grab you in its claws, and drop you into the Tower."

"Then what would happen?" asked Bella, showing nothing but cheerful curiosity.

"That was my job," Gyrod said darkly. "When the progressors are dropped onto the tower, they are dropped into a cage. Guards like me pick them up by one leg, and on that leg they burn a brand onto the ankle, so that they can always be identified as progressors. Then they carry them to the elevators, and they are taken below."

"What's a brand? Does it hurt?" Bella asked, looking up

at the giant's pale glowing eyes.

"Yes."

"How did you lose your job?" Chloe asked sadly.

"There was a lady. A mother clutching an infant. When she was dropped by the harpies, she held the infant tight to protect it, but she fell so far from the harpies' grasp that her legs bent in places legs don't bend. I think if she would have dropped the baby, she would not have broken when she fell. But she didn't drop it, and when I went to her she was unable to stand or crawl away. She tried, pulling herself away from me with one hand, while trying to hold her baby with the other."

Chloe's cheeks were now wet with tears.

"I didn't want to pick the young lady up by her legs, as they looked very precarious. I also feared she would drop the infant, and the new human looked very fragile. So I refused to do my job. I knew this meant I was in trouble, as the captain told me to stand at the wall, so someone else could brand her."

The giant went on, "But there is no sense in refusing to hurt a thing, but then allowing it to be hurt. So I stood with my branding iron between the lady and the other guards." Gyrod sat up tall at this point, and Chloe noticed the color of his eyes had changed from a deep glowing green to a now-defiant orange.

"I pried loose the arms of the first automaton that tried to lift her, and I pulled them from its body. I knocked the second to the ground, and stood on it, which prevented it from reaching her. Then three more lifted me up and threw me over the edge of the Tower. I hung from that spire, there," Gyrod pointed. "I was lucky to have caught myself. But they struck my fingers until my fingers broke," he showed the girls his dented fingers, "and I fell."

"You fell from the top of that Tower?"

"Yes."

"And you are still alive?"

"No." He thought for a moment. "I was never alive, I think. But I am still ticking. Father fixed my gyros and rods, and rewound my main spring. So I am still ticking, and perhaps that's more than I deserve," said Gyrod.

The three sat silent in the cold night air, and watched the specters come and go from the Tower's top.

THE TOYMAKER

When Chloe woke up she could see the striped sheets of Isabella's hammock-bed were in motion. Bella was awake, but not getting up, because it was Chloe's Day.

Chloe could hear Bella, whispering in a sing-songy voice, "Why yes, Mr. Jones, I would love to join the circus." Then in a deeper voice she added, "What tricks can you do?"

Chloe leapt to her feet, expecting to find Isabella playing with stolen toys, but found only corks with faces drawn in pencil and paper dresses. Chloe was disappointed. She would have scolded Bella for taking toys from the toyshop, but she also wanted to see them again.

It had been several days since they had been up in the shop. The girls knew that the brass giant sat up on the workshop table, and knowing they had an audience made them too nervous to risk going up. So Chloe slipped out of bed, and looked for a bag from Uncle James.

The bag sat on the short plank of wood that served as a kitchen counter. It was crumpled, and grease from inside the bag had made the brown paper nearly transparent. She opened it, and found half a loaf of bread, two eggs, a limp and soggy onion, and a piece of sausage about six inches long. There was also a set of eight processed and packaged food bars. These were "full meals" roughly the size of a large brownie. They were distributed by the government in times of food shortages, which was pretty much all the time. Chloe didn't like them, as they had almost no taste, a chalky texture, and after eating them she felt like her tummy was full of dirt. They did however remain edible forever, and were good in a pinch if Uncle James didn't drop by with groceries.

She removed all of this from the bag, and used the bag to start a fire in the stove. While the coals were starting to heat, she put the meal bars on a single board shelf behind the kitchen sink. This shelf was always covered with a fine white powder, plaster-chalk from between the laths of the broken wall it hung on. They only stored packaged food on the shelf, so the fresh foods wouldn't get dusty. The fresh foods they ate right away, which was not a chore, since they never had much.

Chloe fried the sausage. Then she sliced the onions, and scraped them into the pan. After adding all the ingredients, there was not much in the pan, not enough for the girls and their mother.

Chloe frowned.

She walked into the closet with the dirt wall, and picked the last three mushrooms. She hoped there would be more tomorrow.

Back in the kitchen she sliced the mushrooms into quarters, scraped them into the pan, and stirred. There still wasn't enough, so she sliced six slices of the bread, and laid them on three plates. She then put what there was of the omelet between pieces of bread, and carried a plate out of the kitchen.

She handed it to Bella.

"What's this?" Bella asked, looking disapprovingly at the plate.

"Breakfast."

"Breakfast what?"

"Breakfast sandwich."

Bella took the plate with a frown.

"There are also meal bars."

"This looks great. I'll have the sandwich."

Chloe walked back to the kitchen. She filled a glass with water. She opened three bottles of pills, and took two from each bottle and put them on a plate. She then picked up the plate, and the glass of water, and walked out of the kitchen.

Mother's room was dark, and the air smelled like sick. Chloe set the plate and glass on a wooden crate by the bedside, and then turned on the hall light so that she had a little light to work by without the light being too jarring to her mother.

She sat on the bedside, "Mommy? Time for breakfast."

Her mother was still. There was a piece of cloth in her hand, and the rag was mostly speckled red-brown, where her mother often coughed into it. The rag scared Chloe. She had read once that coughing was your body expelling germs, and so Chloe was afraid to touch the rag.

She shook her mothers shoulder gently, and found it warm and moist. "Mommy? Breakfast."

Her mother barely moved.

Chloe put her hand on her mother's forehead, and it was hot.

"Mommy?"

Softly and respectfully, Chloe used one of her tiny thumbs and pulled opened one of mother's eyes slowly.

One ghastly pale eye stared directionless into the room.

Chloe's hand recoiled, and the eyelid shut, too slowly. Mother was still breathing, but she was not responding to anything.

Chloe stood up and left the room. Forgetting her sandwich, she climbed the stairs in the dark, and sat at the top, and cried softly for a short time.

The girls spent the day in their normal routine, working in the schoolbooks Uncle James had smuggled in to them. This was a treat to them, and they worked cheerfully. Schoolwork is something kids hate when they are forced to do it. A child with a choice not to do school loves to do it, and Chloe and Isabella savored it. It made them feel like there was a future for them, and it made them feel like they were real kids. These two things could not have been more important to them.

After school, the girls tried to choke down a meal bar each.

"You'd better save what you don't finish."

"I don't want to. You can have it."

"I don't want it, but you might later. You've hardly eaten anything."

"I'm not hungry for Meal Bar."

"Nobody's ever hungry for Meal Bar." Chloe paused. "You want to listen?"

And so the girls ran to the top of the stairs and were silent. They heard a boy talking.

"Dad, look at this knight! You just speak to him, and he obeys. Watch!"

The boy's voice changed to a taunting sound. "Swing your sword like an idiot!" he said. Then the girls heard the boy laugh in an unfriendly tone.

"I don't like that boy," whispered Isabella.

"Yeah," said Chloe.

Then there was a man's voice. "Justin, have him hit the princess with his sword."

Justin laughed tauntingly, and said, "Run and hit that ugly princess."

Bella stood suddenly, and hit her head on the toyshop floor, and then sat down angrily again.

"I said, hit the ugly princess!" insisted the boy.

There was a moment of silence, and then a small mechanical voice said, "She's not ugly." It was the voice of the knight.

"What did it say?" asked the father. "That's not right," he said, and there was a darkness in his tone that made Chloe feel cold.

"He's refusing!" said the boy. "Can he do that?"

Then Chloe and Bella heard footsteps and the sound of a cane, and they recognized the toymaker's voice.

"I'm sorry sir, but the toyshop is now closed," the toymaker said shortly.

"Are you the toymaker?"

"Yes, I am, and the shop is now closed. Thank you for coming."

"I have a complaint, sir. This toy is an automaton, I assume?"

"I'm sorry, sir, the shop is now closed. We don't take complaints when the shop is closed."

"Sir, my name is Police Inspector Hölzer. Here is my badge." There was a pause. "This toy, as marvelous as it is, appears to be refusing direct instructions."

"Sir," said the toymaker, sounding at once more respectful and more annoyed. "This is just a toy. It is very limited in what it can do."

"But this automation is refusing very particular directions, and it's talking back."

"This toy can't talk," said the toymaker, and if the girls could have seen his face, they would have seen him shoot a disciplining look at the knight.

"It did talk."

"What did you tell the toy to do?"

"Watch. Toy knight, strike the princess with your sword."

Silence.

"Oh!" the boy said in a disappointed tone. "That's not a proper hit!"

The father said, "Sir, you see what I mean? This toy is obviously showing self-interest. And as you know, according to judicial code a122616, no mechanical construct is allowed intelligence beyond the initial purpose of the device."

"The purpose of this device is to be a toy knight that

saves a princess, so hitting the princess would be against its purpose. In addition to that, I have made the play-set not capable of breaking itself. If it could, the toy would be defective. Don't you agree? But sir, the store is now closed. I'm afraid I have to ask you, respectfully, to leave."

"This will call for an investigation."

"That will be fine. Good evening."

There were footsteps, followed by the jingling of bells. The second they heard the bells the two girls, assuming everyone had left the shop, burst through the trapdoor and ran to the cabinet of the knight and princess.

The Princess stood, with arms folded across her miniature chest, glaring angrily at the knight, and she said, "That was foolish. You should have hit me harder."

"But Daisy…" the knight began to reply, but suddenly the toymaker was towering behind the girls and all froze in silence.

"And who have we here? Two little mice from below my floor, I assume?" he had a stern tone, not quite angry, but not happy.

The girls shuddered, and turned slowly around to face him. "Yes, sir."

"And are you allowed to come into my toyshop?"

"No, sir."

The Toymaker bent over and furrowed two bushy white eyebrows at the girls. "And do you sneak into my toyshop after the shop is closed?"

The girls said nothing. Light from a streetlamp outside the windows behind him made the toy master's curly white hair glow translucently, his face framed black beneath it.

"What type of girls would intentionally disobey their good uncle's rules, and put themselves at risk?"

"Bad girls?" Chloe said, her voice choked up. She worked so very hard to be the best girl she could, under very hard circumstances, but always had a horrible fear that she was not good enough, and that's why bad things happened to them. Her eyes filled with tears.

"No, no!" The toymaker said, and he came down on one knee to look her in the eye. "Curious girls, dear one! Curious girls." And he smiled.

Chloe shuddered and cried. It had been a very bad day. The toymaker put his arms around her. "Dear child, don't cry. I'm sorry, I didn't mean to scare you. I'm not good with children. Charlotte wanted–" He stopped, breathed in slowly, and then let the air out just as slowly.

The room was quiet.

Then the toymaker spoke in a more friendly tone, but speaking to the girls as equals. "My name is Calvin. What are your names?" He knew their names.

"I'm Isabella, or Bella or Bella B, or Bee. This is just Chloe," Isabella said proudly.

"Nice to meet you, Isabella. I have an idea. Would you two like to help me in my workshop tonight?"

"Yes!' both girls said at once.

"Aw, good. Come with me!" He led them between the silent silhouettes of a dozen miniature worlds, past the display of massive kites, and to the frosted glass door at the back of the store. It opened with a creak, and he flipped on the light switch.

The brass man sat in the central table, and his glowing eyes darted between the toymaker and the girls. He said nothing.

"No, 'good evening, Father'?" said the toymaker in a teasing voice after the awkward silence.

"Good evening, Father."

"Aw," said the toymaker with a smile, as he walked to a bench to put on a faded leather apron. He took reading glasses from out of the center pocket on his apron, and put them on. Then he placed several small tools into the pocket, and said to the room, "Have you met before?"

"No!" said the brass man, almost before the sentence was out of the toymaker's mouth.

"I see," said the old man, grinning at Gyrod from over the top of his small round spectacles. "Lie down, please."

Gyrod lay down on the workbench as instructed, and Calvin Calgori climbed a small stepladder, so that he could look down at the giant's chest.

Isabella climbed up onto the table, sat on Gyrod's arm, and watched the toymaker unscrew several long, thin brass screws from the giant's chest.

He handed them to Isabella. "Place these in that first dish." He pointed to a series of small wooden bowls on a nearby counter.

"You know, I want to be a doctor when I grow up," Bella said.

"That's a fine thing to be," said Calgori, and he handed

"A doctor that makes sick people better. So if someone can't stop coughing, I could make them stop, and then be happy."

"Oh, I see," said the old man. "That would be a very good thing to be able to do."

For a moment the only sound in the room was the clicking of the toymaker removing the brass man's chest plates.

"And how about you, big sister? What do you want to be when you grow up?"

Chloe was quiet for a moment. She wanted to say, "happy," but that seemed selfish of her, and she felt guilty. "Nothing," she finally said.

"Nothing would be a very bad thing to be. I would not recommend it," said the doctor flatly, almost like a warning. "Is there nothing you've read in your schoolbooks that interests you?"

"Oh, everything interests me!" Chloe said, perking up. "I love math, and writing, especially cursive, which is beautiful. I love drawing beautiful pictures of happy places, and ballerinas! That's what I want to be when I grow up, a ballerina!"

"Have you ever met a ballerina?" The toymaker asked, but as soon as he asked it he regretted it. He knew the answer.

"No," said Chloe quietly.

"I see," said the toymaker. "Maybe I can do something about that."

THE COWBOY

James worked in a very small office in the Tower. The walls were concrete. His desk was dark-green drab-painted metal, held together with rusty rivets. His chair was small, and aluminum, and hard.

He had file cabinets on all four walls, except where the door to the room was, and the cabinets were painted a drab color to match the desk. The cabinets were filled with file after file, each labeled with a person's name. They were color-coded, and a chart on the wall had a colored key to correspond. Green was for "dissenter," purple was for "progressor," red was for "Freelanders' disease," and so on.

A single light bulb hung from a bare cord in the center of the ceiling, and deep inside the nearly windowless tower, its weak light always gave the impression of nighttime.

It was 8:13, and his twelve-hour shift was over. He stood, and pulled out his wallet, and looked at the contents. He had four crumpled one-dollar bills, and three quarters. That would not buy much dinner for his sister and his sister's daughters, let alone his own dinner. So he pulled open his desk drawer, and removed a meal bar, and stuck it in his pocket. This he would eat, and the rest of the money would go to groceries for the girls.

The door to his office swung aggressively open, and hit the file cabinet next to it so hard it rang in his ears. In walked Ian, a tall muscular police officer, redheaded with piercing blue eyes and a muscular physique. Ian was the kind of man who should have been good-looking, but his personality prevented it.

"It smells like a latrine in here. Is that you?" Ian said, placing both hands on James' desk, and glaring at him accusatorially.

"Funny, Ian. That's always funny. Every single time you say it," said James, not quite convincingly. "What can I do for you?"

"Nothing," said Ian. He pulled opening a file cabinet, pulled out a random file, and started reading it, chuckling at the contents.

James folded his arms across his chest, and glanced at the clock. "Then why are you here?"

"Can't a guy visit a friend?" he said, still reading the file. "Ho, ho! This guy didn't go gracefully, did he?"

James walked to Ian and pulled the file out of his hands, and put it back in the cabinet. "That guy had three kids. When he went, the kids went too." James' eyes were red.

Ian looked James in the eye, standing threateningly close, and said, "How's your sister?"

"Audrey's been better," James replied, his voice slow and low. It was a touch gravelly from exhaustion and stress.

"Hey, that's not my fault," Ian said, stepping away. "I've had my hands full just keeping her little secret."

"Yes. You've been great," said James flatly. "It must be exhausting, all that you are doing for them."

"Look, don't guilt me. I gave Audrey a better option when her husband died. But she turned me down."

"You turned down her daughters."

"Hey, those brats aren't mine! It's not my fault Audrey

got knocked up."

James' face turned red, his fists white-knuckled. "Ian, I don't want to start this with you again. I'm tired and I'm going home."

"No, you're not."

"Yes, I am."

"Nope, you're going to this address." Ian pulled a folded file from his back pocket, and threw it on the desk. It was red. At the top of the file was typed, "Jack Kintapush. History of sociopathic abnormalities with a strong possibility of Freelanders' disease."

"Dammit, Ian. I'm tired."

"Yeah, well, you can be as tired as you want, but this guy is smashing faces in a bar eighteen blocks away. So either you go calm him down, or they'll simply turn the idiot off," and Ian laughed. "Frankly, I'd rather you did go home. I haven't drawn my gun in weeks." Ian knew James, and knew James' soft heart would get the better of him.

"Dammit. Alright," James said, and he grabbed his threadbare overcoat.

At the base of the Tower, only a few stories from the ground, a dozen train tracks entered a series of archways into a loading bay. The coal smoke from the trains left long black streaks up the side of the Tower, and filled the boarding platforms with a greasy black fog. James waited for his train to pull to a stop, his coat unable to keep out the chill from the ten-foot fans that tried in vain to remove the coal smoke from the room.

When the train finally stopped, he walked on, and quickly sat on a bench looking out the first window. The train soon filled with angry or tired-looking police officers. Some had helmets and black uniforms with silver armbands depicting a eagle crushing a skull, and a few wore shiny patent-leather hats and black suits, with a similar insignia on their chest pockets.

James wore plain clothes. Old fashioned trousers, long brown overcoat. His job didn't require a uniform, and frankly, he was more effective without one. It was less intimidating.

He watched the city blocks go by, one by one, under the elevated tracks. It was a morose sight, but one he was too familiar with to complain about. When he saw people in the street leaving their first eight-hour job, on their way to a second, all so they could afford to share a cramped apartment with three other families, James did not feel sad for them. He felt envious that he could not give this life to his sister and her daughters.

The citizens of the city all consumed resources from the city: garbage, sewer, food, government services like the police or the hospitals. To limit population, and therefore the consumption of resources, each citizen was assigned consumption points, as long as they were employed. This number was meant to represent how much of the city's resources you were paying back with work, as almost all citizens were employed by the city. 1.5 points were assigned per middle-class working adult. One point for a working child. Zero points were assigned to a non-working adult or child, but each citizen was required to spend one point to pay for their own consumption of resources.

A husband and wife who worked could share their leftover half a point to support one non-working child. When the child reached working age at six years old, that child then earned enough to pay for its own consumption, and the parents could have another child.

If you couldn't cover your child's "consumption points"--say, you'd been too sick for too long--that child would be relocated to another family. At least, that's what you were told. The fact is, once a child was relocated, no family ever saw them again, and the rumors of what actually happened to them were horrendous. The term "relocated" helped calm the families about their children being taken away.

And this is why James hid his sister and her daughters in the basement of the Toyshop. He had known the toymaker, as they had worked together in the Tower for years before the toymaker retired. When Audrey's husband died, leaving her pregnant, and with a toddler, James and Audrey used their extra consumption points to cover the child. When his sister gave birth, and then became sick and could not work, James was forced to hide them, or the children would be taken from Audrey.

He pulled strings with everybody he knew, but in the end, it was Ian who helped him destroy any paperwork relating to Audrey and the girls.

As the train began to slow, James stood up. He pushed his wavy brown hair back, and scratched the back of his neck hard with his fingernails, trying to wake up. He was exhausted in body and soul, but he needed his wits now. His job was never easy.

A line of passengers from the train shuffled, angry and exhausted, down a long zigzagging concrete ramp. Under that ramp was a bar. This was not a nice place. Police officers and other city employees came here to drink government-approved swill, while sitting slumped on hard metal chairs at metal tables. It was dark, and the air was heavy with depression and the smell of cheap government-made liquor.

As James pushed through the crowd, he noticed most of the bar's patrons were standing outside looking in the doors and windows. James watched several of the people jump back, just before a heavy metal barstool came crashing through the front window. Glass from the window jingled around James' battered brown boots.

"Dammit," James mumbled. "This is going to take all night." He walked up to the door. "Jack? Jack Kintapush? Is that you throwing chairs, Jack?"

There was no answer.

James stepped in. He saw overturned tables, broken bottles everywhere, and the floor drenched in liquor. There was a guy on the floor holding a blood-soaked napkin to his broken nose.

James asked, "Jack Kintapush?" The man with the broken nose pointed towards the bar.

At the bar sat a dark man, so still James did not see him at first. He had a long peppered-black braid that reached nearly two-thirds of the way down his long, battered, tooled-leather coat. His hair was shaven on both sides, and his skin was darkened by both ancestry and a life in the sun. His skin was tattooed with images of animals, vehicles, and bones. The tattoos covered his arms, neck and the sides of his head, leaving only his face unadorned.

His face was covered with deep crevices, smile-wrinkles as well as frowns. The wrinkles were deep, but his eyes were deeper still, with brows so heavy that in the dark light of the bar James could not tell if they were open or closed.

James walked slowly towards him. "Jack Kintapush?"

The man was silent.

"Are you Jack Kintapush? Jack, I'm here to help you."

The fan in the ceiling spun slowly, throwing its spinning shadow on the floor.

"You are not going to hurt me, are you, Jack?"

"That depends," Jack said in a voice that sounded like cracked desert clay.

James stopped. "Depends on what?"

"On whether your gonna piss me off or not. I'm not in a great mood, and I'm drunk."

"I noticed that, Jack. I'm James."

"Quit saying my name."

"What?"

"Quit saying my name like you know me. You don't know me. You don't know nothing 'bout me."

"So let's talk."

"I don't feel like talking."

"Look, Jack, do you know who I am?" James now spoke a little more forcefully.

"I think I can guess."

"Then you know what will happen if I can't get you to

talk to me, right?" As James said this, he pulled out a stool two seats from Jack, and sat down.

"I don't care. Unless your gonna get me outta the city, I don't care what happens to me."

"Why would you want to leave the city, Jack? You know how dangerous it is outside the city. Do you want to hurt yourself, Jack?"

"You don't know nothing, do you?" Jack said.

"Jack, outside the city there is nothing."

"Nothing but freedom."

"You know how talking like that makes you sound, Jack? You sound delusional. Sane people don't believe in a magical world outside the city, filled with trees and animals. That's ancient history, Jack. You sound like you have Freelander's Disease."

"Last person who said that to me is bleeding on the floor by the door," Jack said, and he tipped his head toward the man with the broken nose.

"This file they gave me is red, Jack. That means they think you have Freelander's, and they think that because you're talking crazy like this." James set the file on the bar.

"So what now, Jack? What do you think happens from here? Do you think you can just break everyone's noses, and they'll eventually set you outside the city walls to die?"

Jack poured himself a whiskey from a bottle with a government label.

"And then what, you live alone in the rocky wasteland? All alone, until you starve to death?" James said, and he sounded sympathetic when he said it.

"No, James, I would not live alone. I would find my tribe. Find my family. And I would find my horse and my gun, and I would be free again." Jack threw the shot of whiskey down, and poured another. A tear rolled down his cheek, and James saw it and was quiet. "I'm not supposed to be here. I'm supposed to be out there, with my people."

James said sympathetically, "Jack, these are delusions. You were born in the city, and you lived here, just like everybody else. City life has been hard, and you've created these delusions in your head. We all wish there was some magical life somewhere else, but you have to get real, Jack. You can't wish these things into being real. They are only delusions."

"Are they, James? Are these delusions, James? Are these tattoos delusions? Are my clothes delusions?"

"You can wear whatever you want, Jack. "

"Yeah, but could I keep a job with these tattoos? Or with hair this long? How long you think it takes to grow hair this long? Ten years? Twenty? Now, how long do you think a man can be in this city being unemployed, before the police pick him up?"

James was silent. He didn't have an answer for this.

"Who's got the delusion, now?" Jack threw down another shot of whiskey.

James took a deep breath, but then went on in a confident voice. "Alright, so let's play that out. Say the whole city, the whole two million people here are all sharing the same delusion. We all think the world outside the walls is a terrible wasteland, filled with dangers, but we are all crazy…together, living in fear in the city behind a wall? Is that what you think?"

"I only been here four days, but that's about the short of it." Jack was picking at the corner of the now empty whiskey bottle's label, peeling it back.

"And you're saying outside is a paradise, filled with happy people? No dangers?"

"Oh, there's dangers, alright. And hardship. But there aren't no walls, and no rules, 'cept the rules of survival and friendship and family. Those walls you think you're hiding behind ain't there to keep monsters out, they're there to keep you in. Those guns on the wall ain't there to keep the beasts away, they're there to shoot people who try to escape. There's a whole world outside the city you've never seen, and you're not allowed to see, because once the people of this city saw that world, they would tear down the walls, guns or no. It's a world of space, and nature, and the last of the free people."

Jack had now peeled the label back from the whiskey bottle, and he handed it to James. Under the government label was another faded label, hand-printed, that read, "Blackfoot Whiskey, Distilled Nomadically by the Last of The Free People."

James stood up and dropped the bottle.

THE BALLERINA

Things were now different after nightfall in the toyshop. Since they had befriended the toymaker, the little girls came up each night, and each night he greeted them. He would show them toys he had made, and he would teach them how the toys worked, and as he did, he would play with them, and tell them about the world.

"These are the trains that bring the food to the city from all over the world," Calvin said, turning a dial that made a set of ornate electric trains puff across a miniature diorama of a city like the one they lived in. There was a tall wall surrounding the city, and nothing but gravel fields outside it.

"Where do they get the food?" asked Isabella.

"Secret farms and ranches outside the city walls."

"But I thought there was nothing outside the walls but rocks, and monsters," Isabella said.

"Did you?" Calvin moved to the diorama on a different cabinet. "They do say that, don't they? This is an Aeroflet," said Calvin, switching on an eight-inch flying platform, on which little mechanical men stood with rifles. "Hunters stand on these platforms to shoot the beasts as they run around in the jungle."

"Oh, that's horrible!" said Chloe, shooing a half dozen small mechanical tigers into a cluster of tiny trees, and out of range of the miniature hunters.

"It is?" said, Calgori. "Aw, well then," and he reached

into another toy display, and pulled what looked like a beautifully ornate pirate ship hanging from under a Zeppelin. He placed it above the hovering model of the aeroflet. "Then these will be airship pirates, and they will attack the hunters."

The rather large miniature airship swung around mid-air to point its broadside at the aeroflet. Its cannon shot out little streams of sparks towards the hunters on the platform, and as it did, Calvin made booming noises with his mouth, as a small boy would.

"Airship pirates hate the hunters," Calvin said.

"Why?" asked Isabella.

"The hunters on the platform work for the City. The City tries to lock the pirates in the Tower. Airship pirates want to live free outside the City, with the nomads, and the Sea Gypsies, but it's against the law."

"Calvin?" Chloe asked.

"Yes, Chloe?"

"Is that for pretend? Is that just a pretend while playing with the toys, or is there really a jungle outside the city, and pirates and Indians, and Gypsies, and animals?"

The toymaker turned to Chloe and Isabella, and thought a moment about how he should answer. Then he said, "The schools here would teach you it is a pretend. Your uncle would tell you it was a pretend. Maybe it is just a pretend. Maybe it's just a dream, and maybe if you chase your dreams people will call you crazy. Many people have called me crazy about many things they didn't believe in, until I built those things. In the end, when I was right, they never saw what I did. They went on thinking my dreams wouldn't work long after I proved it to them, and they went on thinking I was crazy. But I was happy being right, all the same."

But he looked dark and distant, not happy.

Chloe thought, he didn't answer my question. Maybe he didn't want to.

Then a sparkle came into Calvin's eyes, as he seemed to remember something. "Chloe, I made you something. Would you like to see it? It's very wonderful."

"Oh, please!" Chloe said.

"It's in the workshop," he said, and he walked briskly, like a little boy on Christmas morning.

The inside of the workshop was dark, and Gyrod was standing to one side of the workbench, looking reverentially towards it. On the bench was a seated figure draped in a white sheet.

"Is it a toy ghost?" Bella said, clearly excited about the prospect.

"No, it's better than that," said Calvin. "But stay right there, she's not quite done, and I don't want to scare you. Or you her." He quickly put on his leather apron. "This will only take a minute."

Calvin lifted something from the counter that looked like a lumpy pearl-white dish, with several holes in it. It was flexible in his hands as he carried it to the shop table. He slid the sheet down, but blocked what was under it with his shoulders, while he attached the dish. He then pulled the sheet back up, and went around to the back of the figure.

There was a ratcheting sound, as Clavin wound the

large toy, and when he stopped, Chloe could hear a soft whirring noise. Then Calvin snapped a rear panel in place, and the noise was muted.

At once the figure under the sheet moved, straightening its posture, and turning its head.

It was alive.

"I… There is something wrong. I can't see," said a small, timid female voice from under the sheet. "Hello? Is there anyone there?"

Bella stepped towards the workbench. "It's because you're under covers."

"Oh." The voice seemed surprised. "I see. May I remove them?" asked the voice.

"Feel free," said Calvin, who was now on the far side of the shop hanging a few small tools back in their place on the wall.

Two delicate arms reached out from under the sheet, and slowly pulled it down, revealing the face of a beautiful teenaged girl. She had brown hair pulled back into a bun, large moist dark eyes and soft white skin. She held the sheet around herself at her shoulders, and she looked shy.

Her skin and eyes were flawless. You would not have been able to tell her from a real girl, if not for a few not-yet-concealed joints and gears around her elbows and neck. Calgori intended to cover those, but he was concerned that she would look too real, and would therefore be illegal. Out of fear of the social ramifications of sentient machines, the government had outlawed all but the simplest of automatons. This posed a problem for automatons, because none were actually simple enough to adhere to the law, so they all hid their intelligence. Exposed gears helped them to look primitive.

"I'm cold," she said. "And... scared." The sheet was quivering, as were her long slender legs now protruding from under it.

"You're not cold. Your body is telling you that you're naked." Calvin came over and held out to her a small pile of pale blue silk. "Put this on." He had a very sympathetic tone in his voice, and this worried Chloe.

The girl brushed the sheet aside with one arm, and she was indeed naked. Her face was full of shame and fear, and she glanced around the room nervously and abashedly. She had the body of a slender girl of seventeen, all ribs and nearly flat chest, and she crossed her arms across her chest to hide her small breasts.

She took the garment from Calgori, and she stepped off the worktable with a surprisingly graceful and intentional movement. She stepped into it, pulled it up to her waist, and then pulled her arms through the shoulder straps.

With the dress on, Chloe and Isabella jumped and clapped. "A ballerina!" they exclaimed, as the girl was indeed wearing a leotard and a tutu. The Ballerina stared questioningly at the girls.

Calvin got down on one knee in front of Chloe. "Weeks ago you told me you wanted to be a ballerina when you grew up. So I made you a ballet teacher."

Chloe hugged him, a huge smile stretching across her face.

At "made you," the ballerina looked again at her arms and legs, which were perfectly formed and covered with goose bumps. Then she looked at Gyrod, and tried not to look horrified when she looked back at the joints in her own arms.

Calvin stood up, and turned toward the ballerina. "Your name is Timony. I am Doctor Calvin Calgori. This is Isabella, and Chloe. You are to teach them ballet. Would you like to do that?"

"Do I know ballet?" asked Timony, looking surprised.

"You do," said Calvin. "Why don't you curtsy?"

She gazed blankly for just a second, as if trying to remember something, and a small clinking sound came from her chest. Then she curtsied, slowly and gracefully, with a good deal more flourish than she expected. Timony was surprised, but her motions were polished and perfect.

Chloe and Bella curtsied back, much less gracefully but with huge smiles. "She's the most beautiful ballerina I have ever seen!" Bella said.

Then Timony looked worried. "Doctor?"

"Yes, Timony?" Calgori said.

"I… I can't… remember anything." Her eyes widened, and she looked at him imploringly. "I think there is something wrong."

"No, there is nothing wrong, Timony. You can't remember anything because you've just been born. Just this minute. There is nothing yet to remember."

Timony looked horrified, and she looked down at her

legs, and held out her arms, and began to tremble.

"I know, it's confusing."

Gyrod stepped forward now, and stood over her. In his deep, scratchy voice he said, "I was scared too, Timony, at first."

Timony looked up at the giant with wide eyes, and then back to Calgori imploringly.

"Please sit down, Timony," said the doctor. "I'm afraid it's always a bit of a shock, but better that shock than never to have been born." He said this more to himself than her, as if to reassure himself. Timony looked scared, and she sat down once again on the workbench.

Calvin said, "I'm afraid it's always worse, the more intelligent you are. Try not to let it get to you." He sighed and looked sympathetic. "Much of what you know has been copied from elsewhere. This is how you can walk, and talk, and dance, and think. You remember what a table is, and what a door is, but I can't give you personal memories. That leads to all kinds of sadness. When I've done that in the past the poor souls felt ripped from another life... one they had not actually lived, and they spend all their waking hours trying to get back to loved ones they never knew."

Timony was crying now. Small silver tears ran down pearly-white soft cheeks. Deep inside her porcelain head, she thought it would be better to miss loved ones, to miss a mommy, than never to have one.

Calgori gave her a fatherly hug. Then he said, "I think you'd feel better if you danced. When things feel strange, doing that which you were made to do will make them feel normal again." Timony looked up into his eyes, and he kissed her on the forehead.

The old man walked to the corner of the room, shoulders slumped and tired. He placed an old lacquer disk on a very old-looking Victrola, and turned the crank. He pointed its beautiful brass horn toward the center of the room, and placed the needle on the record. The machine began to play a crackling but beautiful waltz, and the two small girls bounced on their feet a bit to the music, barely able to contain themselves. They had not heard much music before, in their silent apartment below the toyshop, so this was a wonderful treat.

Timony, still looking scared and nervous, took three steps towards the center of the room. Without trying, the steps fell perfectly in time to the 3/4 rhythm of the waltz.

"There you are," said the old man. "I'm afraid I only have a few records… I'll need to find you some Strauss or Tchaikovsky. But this will have to do for now."

Timony held her left arm low and curved, and her right arm higher so that her hand was level with her head. She took two steps and a shuffle, once again her feet falling effortlessly in time to the music.

Then she smiled, for the first time in her life. The doctor was right. This is what made her feel happy, and her smile made him smile.

She turned to Chloe, and waved her over with one hand. Timony placed one arm around the small of Chloe's back, held her other hand up high, and with a nod that meant, now we'll begin, Timony waltzed Chloe around the room. Chloe beamed, and grinned so wide you could see all of her teeth, her pigtails bouncing and swinging to the

music. They spun around the workshop. Timony looked
content and perfectly at home, back arched gracefully, red
lips slightly parted, eyes no longer moist, but smiling.

Little Isabella bounced on her toes, raising one hand,
and said, "Oh, my turn! My turn!" So the good doctor

walked across the floor, took her by both hands, and put her feet atop his. Then he waltzed her, in smaller circles and clumsier than the elegant Timony, but all smiled and laughed as the scratchy Victrola squealed out its Viennese waltz.

Now, children have a gift. You know this, if you can remember it, though many lose the memory early on. Children can be happy in the hardest of circumstances. Their happiness is simply relative, since they don't have many experiences to tell them about the unfairness of their life. So when you might say to yourself, "It's not fair I don't have luxuries that others have," and you might get horribly unhappy about it, a small child will think, "I'm so lucky to have found a rock shaped like a horse!" and play happily with it all day. Their joy is simply relative to the rest of their lives, and so even Chloe and Isabella had been happy many times before.

But this dance was the deepest, and most profound happiness they had yet felt. There was no fear, and no worry, and no foreboding in this. It seemed to them as though their life had taken a huge and permanent step towards a happier life.

Which is why I'm so sorry to tell you about what is to come.

STOLEN

After the dance had ended, as the record repeated a skipping scratch at the center of the disk. Gyrod mumbled something under his breath, and he did so more to himself than anyone else.

"I beg your pardon, what was that?" asked Doctor Calgori as he lifted the needle, silencing the Victrola.

"I," Gyrod's voice droned, "I was wondering…that is…" He seemed shy to ask the question, but Calgori came to him with a smile and put his hand on the giant's knee.

"Well, if I was built to do bad things…" Gyrod looked mournful, "…but I refuse to do bad things, then what do I do when things seem strange? You told Timony to do what she was made to do, and that would make her happy. How do I do what I was meant to do, and feel happy, like Timony?"

"I see," said Calgori, and he took off his glasses and cleaned them with a handkerchief. After a moment, he put them back on, and said, "Perhaps we need to give you a new purpose." The toymaker smiled, and Gyrod sat up a bit. "Perhaps you should be a–" Calvin was interrupted by a crash, and broken glass scattered across the floor out in the toyshop.

The children ran to each other, and then looked to Calvin. Calvin strode to a window between the workshop and the toy store. It was a one-way mirror-window he used to keep an eye on the shop while working on his toys. From the toy store, it looked like a mirror hung on the wall. Calvin's brow furrowed, and his face turned red at what he saw.

Police officers appeared at the front of the shop, their shiny black boots crunching in the needlessly broken glass of the front door. One officer stood giving orders, while several others were clumsily filling sacks with toys.

"They'll break!" said Chloe, now at the window by Calvin, looking very distressed at the abuse of the fragile toys.

Gyrod stood up, all eight feet of him, stooping slightly because of the ceiling, and clutching one huge metal fist around a wooden pillar in the center of the room.

"No, Gyrod," said the toymaker. "Stay hidden. This won't go well for any of us if they come back here and find you and Timony and the girls." Calvin exhaled deeply and slowly, and then added, "I will handle this."

He took a deep breath, then opened the door to the shop. He stood tall and confident, and asked, "What is the meaning of this?" He was addressing the officer in charge, and he recognized him as the father who complained to him about the toys a few nights ago.

"Calvin Calgori," the officer said with a tone of victory. "I'm placing you under arrest. The court has found you guilty of creating illegal toys. You shall be taken to The Cage for re-education, and your toys will be impounded, and destroyed," said the officer in a gloating voice, and he smiled broadly as he did.

Calvin was silent. His hands quivered at his side. It was strange for Gyrod to see his father as anything but strong and confident, and Calgori was obviously scared. He spoke in a quivering voice, "Then let me get my cane, it's just inside the door here."

He stepped quickly back into the workshop, and grabbed his cane without making eye contact with anyone in the workshop. Then he flicked off the lights, and just before backing out of the room he whispered quickly, "Gyrod, here is your purpose. You look after these girls. Look after them, until they have a father again. Take the girls, and Timony, and hide." He closed the door then, and locked it.

Then he hobbled back out of the workshop, and shut the door. Isabella ran forward in the dark, and locked the door, then ran back and stood between Gyrod's legs, holding Chloe's hand.

The toymaker walked slowly on his cane back to the officer, and while he did so, he secretly handed the workshop key to the toy knight. The knight walked unseen with the key to the dragon, and the dragon took it from him, and swallowed it.

"Honestly, officer, your people come here every five years, and cause a big mess. I don't so much mind the accusations, which I'm always exonerated of, I might add, but the damage you do is truly a bother." He spoke as if this was a mere inconvenience, but his hands were still shaking.

"Not this time, Doctor Calgori," said the officer darkly. "The laws have changed. If you're accused of the same crime more than three times, even if you've been exonerated in the past, you will now be punished for the crime." The officer grinned. "You are abusing the city's resources by this frequent waste of the court's and the police department's time."

"Oh, is that how they've chosen to label this?" Calgori snarled back. "Why don't they just admit they need my services again?"

Chloe and Bella could hear nothing of this, as they watched with the automatons through the one-way glass. They saw the toymaker arguing with the officer, and then they saw the officer grab Calgori by the arm and drag him out to the street. Calgori looked terrified now, and he was looking skyward in horror. He struggled, and tried to break free of the officers' grip, but this only caused the officer to hit him in the thigh with his cudgel, knocking the old man to his knees. Poor old Calvin cried out in pain at this.

Then a shadow fell over the toymaker, and he looked into the sky and covered his face with his arms. Chloe screamed as a massive brass skeleton descended from the sky and clasped its oversized hands around the doctor's waist. This phantom hung from its own small zeppelin, and its glowing red eyes darted around the street as it held its prey. Then it leapt up again from the street and disappeared from view, taking Calgori with it.

The two little girls cried as quietly as they could, and turned to Gyrod. They hugged his legs, and buried their faces in the cold metal of his thighs.

The wooden pillar Gyrod had been holding now splintered and crushed in the grip of his silent rage. In another second he would have leapt from the toyshop and pursued his father, but the girls clung to him in terror, now crying loudly. The two remaining guards in the toyshop looked up from their jobs of collecting the toys, and stared towards the workshop door.

Gyrod's eyes turned blue and narrowed with worry. He stooped close to Chloe and Bella, and put his fingers in front of his lips. "Let us leave, as quickly and quietly as we can." And the giant, the ballerina, and the two little girls slipped silently up the spiral staircase and into Calgori's apartment.

Now I only know about this next part because a toy told the girls later, and they told me. Neither Timony, nor Gyrod, nor the two little girls were aware of this at the time, but it's so wonderful I have to tell you about it.

As the automatons and the children slipped unseen into the toymaker's apartment, only two police offers were left in the shop, their superior having left shortly after Calvin had been taken into custody. Finding the workshop door locked, these two officers began to trample small mechanical animals, and thrust the beautiful princesses roughly into their large sacks, until the remaining toys could not endure it any longer.

All at once there was small battle cry from a hundred toy soldiers, and a war against wicked giants began.

The first to engage the giants were the airship pirates. If you know half as much about airship pirates as I do, this won't surprise you at all. Their zeppelin throttled its sputtering propellers until they were level between the two giants' inattentive heads, and they fired port and starboard broadsides straight into their faces. Now miniature cannon have miniature cannonballs, and these were designed as toys. However, the Toymaker was not too concerned with safety, having made the toys more for himself than for kids, and so the marble-sized cannonballs hit the giants with

roughly the same force as a marble thrown by an angry twelve-year-old bully.

Which is to say, it hurt a lot.

The officers were thrown completely off their guard and tried to cover their faces, but as they did, the next wave assaulted them. One hundred toy soldiers opened fire from the ground, pelting them with bullets the size of the tip of a needle. These bullets penetrated the officers' trousers and pierced their skin like a hundred bee stings. One of the officers–the smaller one–at this point dropped his bag and ran out of the shop screaming in a most embarrassingly high-pitched voice.

The other, a large angry man with a ridiculously large blond mustache, kicked out with his boot and launched a dozen soldiers into the air. These soldiers hit the cabinet behind them and snapped into pieces. He then swung his bag of toys like an evil Santa, and hit the airship out of the sky. It crashed into a toy castle across the room, and many pirates fell to their death.

The evil Santa smiled smugly, and turned to leave, but as he did so, he found himself face to face with a large copper and brass scaled dragon, a miniature princess riding just behind its ears. It glared down at him like a wicked gargoyle from the top of a large toy building.

The princess yelled, "Lunge!" and the beast leapt from the top of the four-foot skyscraper, landing brass tooth and brass claw into the guard's face. The guard thrashed in vain, as the dragon clawed at his face and ears. Finally wrenching the dragon from his face, the guard ran from the toyshop.

The toys were victorious.

BROKEN TOYS

Although neither of the original police officers were willing to return to the toyshop, more were sent. Seeing the many wounds of their fellow officers, eight officers returned with helmets and shields, and two automaton guards of the same make as Gyrod. I won't tell you about their collection, as it was too horrible to report. Many toys were broken beyond repair in that battle.

Gyrod and Timony and the girls had been hiding on the roof top, but they came back to the shop just before dawn, and found a miniature wasteland. Buildings were smashed, airships crushed, and not a single toy soldier or pirate was left. In fact, the only toys not destroyed were the simplest ones: balls, kites, rollerskates. Almost nothing that could walk or talk or play back with you was left alive, and the few that were didn't live past telling the story of the toy battle to Chloe and Bella.

The girls cried, as you would have if you'd seen countless friends lying crushed on the ground. Timony sat, legs crossed, and held the girls as they cried. Gyrod stepped gingerly around the room, looking for anyone he might help. He found only one toy still moving. A small circus elephant was hiding under a discarded battleship. Gyrod picked it delicately from the wreckage with his massive hands, and carried it back to the girls. The elephant ran into Isabel's open arms like a miniature puppy would, and wrapped its small trunk around her tiny wrist for reassurance.

"The sun will rise soon," Gyrod said with a tone of concern. "You should go home."

84

"But where will you hide, Gyrod?" Isabella asked.

"I am not sure," he said nervously. "I think I must hide in the city, somewhere dark. I am not supposed to be—" he searched for the words, and finally settled on "I am not supposed to be."

"Stay with us!" The girls implored.

"I should find James."

All was forebodingly quiet, and then he spoke again. "Timony, you may stay here if you'd like. If you clean the shop, and the police come back, you will look like a regular worker. Tell the police Doctor Calgori built you to help, and you will stay and clean the shop." Then he looked her urgently in the eye, "It's very important you don't look like you can think for yourself, or care about what happens to you. It's too complicated to explain now, but try to act like a machine." Then Gyrod stood, and he walked to the door to leave, but as the early morning sun began to lighten the street behind him he turned and said, "I will be back tonight. I will take care of you. Stay hidden."

And so the girls returned to their dark and dusty apartment below the stairs. Instead of climbing into their bunks, they went into their mother's room, and climbed into her bed. She did not wake, but they held each other and cried, and when exhaustion was greater than sadness, they fell asleep.

SILENCE ABOVE

In the afternoon they woke, and the girls sat on the stairs in quiet conversation. There was no sound above, and the silence was terrifying.

So they whispered, "There are no kids playing today."

"No, and no toys," Chloe said sadly.

"Do you think Calgori was eaten by the skeleton?" asked Isabella, her eyes red and fearful.

"I don't think so. Automatons don't eat, as far as I know," said Chloe. "I think he was taken to the Tower."

"I wish we had a hero to rescue him. Like when a princess is taken to a tower."

"I wish we had a hero to rescue us," said Chloe. "But I don't even know what a 'rescue' would mean for us."

"What did Gyrod mean, when he told the ballerina to act like a machine?"

"I don't know. It sounds like it is against the law to be a thinking automaton. That's why they took the toys that could play with you, but left the toys that couldn't, like the kites." Chloe sat and thought a moment. "It feels like most good things are against the law."

"Yeah," said Isabella.

"It's still quiet. Wouldn't the kids come anyway? I mean, if the door is broken, and the other toys are just lying around, wouldn't the kids come in and at least play with the other toys?" asked Isabella. "What do you think the quiet signal flies?"

"I think it sig-ni-fies..." she pronounced this word slowly, to instruct Bella, "...that the kids are scared to come. They know something bad happened here, and so they are staying away."

Above them in the shop, Timony spent the day cleaning solemnly. She had never cleaned before, and she was not good at it. But her goal was not to make a clean room. She had seen how sad the girls were at seeing the broken dolls, and so she wanted to clean away the little bodies so the girls would not have to see them. More than once she shivered, as she picked up a tiny body and realized that she was no different than these broken toys.

So Timony swept, and while she swept she worried about the girls, and how to get them food. She had no money, and didn't know how she could earn it, since automatons apparently only worked for people who owned them, and were not paid.

Most of the day, the street outside the shop was filled with commuters, doing their best not to look at the shop. They knew the shop well, and anyone who had regularly passed the shop had long suspected that the magic in the shop was not legal. The broken glass and missing toys and official red signs posted to the windows were proof that the police had caught up with the eccentric toymaker.

By the early evening, Timony had managed to put the shop in order enough so that a drunk man staggering from one bar to another mistook the shop as open.

He staggered into the shop, and saw the destruction, and said in an inappropriately loud voice, "Geez, this place is a dump!"

Then he saw Timony. She was on the far side of the room sweeping. Her small and symmetrical back was to him.

"Hey there, barmaid, how's'about'a drink?" he slurred, walking towards her. He was a heavier man, with a red nose and a tight brown velvet suit jacket, the buttons of which were barely containing his alcohol-engorged stomach.

Timony stopped sweeping, and turned slowly and gracefully to face him. "A drink?" she asked.

"Ho, ho!" he said, seeing how pretty she was. His eyes traced the outline of her barely pubescent figure. He licked his lips.

"I am not a barmaid," she said, and she furrowed her brow and looked sternly at him. She was angry at him for staggering disrespectfully around this solemn scene, and she pursed her lips, frowning.

He didn't see anger. He saw a tease. He saw a pretty girl playing "hard to get."

"No, you're not a barmaid!" he laughed loudly, and grabbed her tutu. "You're a dancer!" he said, walking around behind her. He slid a thick hand over one of her shoulders, and caressed her exposed collarbone.

She stood still, confused. "Yes. I am."

"I'll bet you just love to dance," he said, his voice filled with greasy innuendo.

"I do," she said solemnly. "It makes me happy."

"Oh, I bet it makes everyone happy," he chuckled, and he put his hands on her hips. "Will you dance with me?"

"I have to clean this shop."

"Why don't you clean afterward? That'd make more sense, wouldn't it?" he said softly and uncomfortably close to her ear. "How much you cost?"

Timony thought about the girls, and getting them food. She didn't understand what this awful man wanted her to do, but she knew he meant to pay her for it, so she said, "Twenty-five."

THE KITCHEN FLOOR

Chloe woke in the morning, and all was quiet. She could see Isabella's small pink hand dangling off the side of the hammock, and knew she was still sound asleep.

Chloe slipped her feet off the bed onto the cold and dusty stone floor. She rubbed her eyes with two fists, and felt the grainy sleep sand.

She sat on the raggedy bedside, letting her eyes open and close. Finally she stood, and trudged slowly to the kitchen, shuffling her feet as she went.

She looked at the kitchen counter. It was bare. No paper bag. She frowned in a defeated way, and glanced towards Mother's room. She went to the sink and poured a glass of water. The water was brownish-orange, so she dumped it out, and then filled it again. This time, the water was clearer, so she set it on the counter, pulled a plate from the sink, and washed it. She put a meal bar on the plate–it was the second to the last–and she picked up the plate and the glass and carried them to Mother's room.

The first thing she saw was that mother's handkerchief appeared to be muddy. It was completely covered with dark brown, and there were dark brown spots on the blankets as well.

She looked at mother's face, and for an instant Chloe was mad. It looked to her as though Isabella had put purple lipstick on Mother's lips as she slept, and that seemed horribly disrespectful. But then Chloe noticed that mother's cheeks looked wrong. They looked more limp than the night before, and more transparent.

Chloe set the glass and plate on the nightstand, and put her hand on her mother's forehead. But instead of being startlingly hot, it was ice-cold.

Chloe took a slow step backward. Her vision was

blurring at the sides, and her face and chest were getting painfully tight. Her mind was trying to fight off a realization of what had happened, but the realization was coming anyway. She frowned uncomfortably hard, and bit her lower lip, and ran out of the room.

Chloe could barely see now, her eyes were so wet, and she fell to her knees in the kitchen. She curled up in a ball at the base of the kitchen sink, and stared at her toes, and watched them blur until she could not recognize them.

Hot tears burst from her eyes, and ran down her cheeks. And then she cried. It burst out of her. Her mouth fell open, her lower lip trembled, and she cried, and screamed, and cried some more.

Isabella woke to the sound of Chloe's crying. Instinctively she knew what must have happened, so she ran past Mother's room, not daring to look in. She ran to the kitchen, and buried her face in Chloe's lap, and she cried too.

They cried until they were exhausted from crying, until the sadness was drowned out by the physical exhaustion of the tears. And when they had no strength left for crying, they sat panting, and sobbing, two silhouettes holding each other on the dark and dirty kitchen floor.

There were footsteps on the basement stairs, a single set of hard-soled shoes. They heard the footsteps cross the living room floor and stop at mother's doorway a moment. And they heard a man catch his breath.

A scratchy voice said softly, "Oh, girls!" It was their

uncle, James! And Gyrod behind him. They ran to James, and they hugged him around the waist, and they all cried again, and James sat on the floor of the hall outside his sister's bedroom, and he held the girls.

ODD FOOD

Later that night, James said to the girls, "you two girls try to eat something." He handed them a small brown paper bag. He had a frantic look in his eyes. It was not sadness, but fear and desperation.

"I'll be back as soon as I can manage, but I have to go take care of things," and he left the girls. Gyrod followed him, carrying Mother's body from their basement apartment. Chloe was grateful that Mother's face was under a sheet.

The apartment was empty, cold and silent. The quiet felt heavy, as if the air was somehow thicker.

There were no sounds from the shop, no children playing. No Uncle James, no toymaker, no Gyrod, no Timony. Not even the sound of Mother sleeping in the other room. The small basement apartment was quieter than the girls had ever heard before.

There was not much in the bag. Three meal bars, and the girls weren't hungry. They felt trapped now, more than they ever had felt before. Without mother sleeping in the other room it felt as if it was now up to the girls to look to the future more than ever before. Before there had at least been a faint glimmer of hope that mother would wake at smile, and be better.

Now there was no hope.

"Now that Mother is gone, who is to look after us?" Bella asked Chloe. She was sitting on the dusty floor looking at her dirty, too-tight shoes.

"I'm not sure," said Chloe, knowing that it was they who had taken care of their mother most of Isabella's life.

"Why doesn't Uncle James take care of us?" Isabella asked.

"He tries, but he has to work," Chloe said. "He works all the day, and most of the night. I don't think he'd have time to be here at all. Besides, he has to keep us a secret. If he came here every day, the secret would be discovered."

The truth was that Uncle James, being only one man, did not have enough consumption points to legally keep the girls. He would have to keep them hidden, alone in the basement apartment. But the girls new nothing of this.

They discussed their fate most of the evening in worried tones, until it was late night. But just as they were thinking of going to bed, so tired that they were close to falling asleep where they sat, they heard a sound, the sound of the trap door, followed by light and graceful footsteps on the stairs.

"Little girls?" said Timony, calling from the stairs. The girls jumped up, and ran and hugged her, and were so glad to have a friend.

Timony held a very large paper bag in her arms, and she set it on the old bench that served as a table in the center room of the apartment.

"I've brought you food," she said in a forced cheerful tone. She seemed very tired and dirty and sweaty.

"I didn't know you could sweat," Isabella said.

"It's not my sweat," answered Timony, but the girls didn't quite understand as they were enthralled with

95

the grocery bag. They ripped into it like you might have unwrapped Christmas presents when you were a small child. The contents were unexpected. There were radishes, onions, chewing tobacco, mustard, a brick of blue cheese, sugar cubes, a jar of oregano, and some tape. Timony had never eaten, or even seen a meal, so she didn't understand anything about it.

With each new item the girls' excitement was replaced with a look of puzzlement, as they tried to picture how they could arrange this odd assortment into a meal.

Timony could see the expression on their faces, and she sighed, and said, "What did I do wrong?"

"None of this is food that–" Bella started to say, but Chloe interrupted. Chloe had noticed that Timony's tutu was filthy, and torn, with strange stains in spots, and that the ballerina's hair was disheveled and torn.

So Chloe said, "Nothing's wrong, this is wonderful." And she tore off a mouthful of bitter blue cheese, trying her best to swallow it without spitting it back up. She shuddered as she swallowed.

"I can get more. Or something different," Timony said, but she looked scared when she said it. She looked at the girls imploringly, fearful of what she must do to earn more money.

"Maybe we can make you a list," Bella began to say, but Chloe added, "This will last a while. Thank you so much."

Bella gave Chloe a look that said, Why would you tell her that, if she could get more?

And Chloe flashed her back a glance that said, Shush! I'll tell you later!

And so Isabella had a dinner of radishes, and Chloe had a dinner of blue cheese and sugar cubes (to make it less bitter). Finally the three went to sleep, Chloe in her bed, Bella in her hammock and Timony lying battered on the floor in the corner of their room, looking like the broken doll that she was.

THE VIEW

When James and Gyrod left the apartment the night of Audrey's death, the streets were dark and a fog obscured everything. The fog was so thick that from one side of the street they could not see the buildings on the other side.

This was fortunate for the small man and the brass giant. When they saw a policeman or automaton patrol far down the cobblestone alleys, they could avoid getting close enough to be seen carrying the body of Audrey.

James had a dilemma. He could not take his sister's body to a morgue, as he would have to explain her. He had had the records for Audrey and the children destroyed, and so her body would be very hard to explain. This would lead to an investigation, which might lead to the children, which would in turn lead to their incarceration, or worse, "relocation." No one ever was heard from again after "relocation."

James led Gyrod down many blocks of the city. Some were empty, containing only the sound of their feet on the coal-stained stones. Others were filled with hustling commuters leaving their evening jobs and heading home or to a night job. The commuters' eyes were nearly always on their feet, but when they did see the brass giant holding a body, they quickly looked away. I saw nothing!

Finally, they came to the Wall. It loomed above them, dark, and foreboding, and filthy black. It seemed to say, This is the end. You cannot pass me, as there is no more world after me. This was a little-frequented part of town, and James chose this spot because he knew the guard who worked this section of the wall, and knew that the guard was a drunk. By now, he would be fast asleep in his tower, and James and Gyrod could climb the wall unseen.

There was an iron staircase, with a locked gate at the bottom.

"Gyrod, can you get through that lock?" James asked.

The giant shifted the body over to one arm, and reached out his other hand. He pinched the lock between his thumb and fore-finger, and crushed it as easily as you might crush a peanut.

James opened the rusty cast-iron gate, revealing a metal stairway like a fire escape. It led up several flights to a set of more substantial concrete stairs.

Up they climbed, flight after flight, and soon James could not see the ground through the midnight black fog. All he could hear was the distant sound of a steam train. There was now fog above and below them, and the Wall disappeared from sight in both directions. James' legs ached.

But they climbed onward still, many more flights, and as they climbed, it became lighter, and the fog thinner, and before long, they could see the top of the wall above them, and the early beginnings of a golden sunrise in the sky above them.

"We've got to hurry, Gyrod. We have to get back into the City before it's light enough for us to be seen," said James, and he pushed his aching legs into one last effort.

At last they reached the top of the Wall. Looking down its length they could see guard towers, with their searchlights and guns. Looking into the city, they could see building tops poking out of the clouds of thick fog, that now seemed held within the wall like soup in a pot.

But as James looked away from the City, he was struck dumb. He was looking out of the city for the first time in his life, and saw the sun was rising fast, illuminating a vast forest. Treetop after treetop stretched for miles, the canopy only breaking for little rivers and swamps. He could see the heads of tall beasts between the trees, feeding peacefully on their leaves, and he could see flocks of birds darting in the sky above them. Far off above the horizon, he saw the silhouette of an airship: a balloon the shape of football, with an old-fashioned sailing ship's hull hanging below it.

There was simply no way to trick his mind into continuing with his old beliefs. The City was no longer the whole world, and outside the City was no longer just cold stone and death. This was the world, this sea of trees, and rivers, and animals, and freedom.

The only cold stone and death were inside the city walls.

James thought of Jack Kintapush, and his sadness at being torn from this world outside. He looked with tears of confusion and joy at the ground, hoping to see Jack running from the walls, or see Jack's tribe's caravan coming to the rescue. Of course James saw neither of these things. He was tired now, and his mind was wandering.

Then James remembered the two little girls, and as he did, he looked out over the trees to the swamp beyond, and, almost beyond the limit of his sight, he saw what appeared to be a tiny cabin on a dock in the middle of a marsh.

He looked down the outside of the Wall on which they stood, trying to find a way out. But there were no stairs, and no ladders, and no doors. Just a sheer drop of hundreds of

feet. Falling from such a height would be certain death.

So then James closed his eyes, and after a moment of silence, he nodded, Gyrod knelt and released Audrey's body, letting it drop from the Wall, into the forest far below.

BOOTSTEPS

The next day James returned, and was surprised to find Timony in the apartment. He had never met the young ballerina before, and after some explaining, he accepted her presence, and then ignored her.

"I'm so sorry girls," he said, as he hugged them. He had a panicked look in his eyes.

"I've brought no food. I've been up all night, and my mind is blurry and confused. I've had one shock after another, and I need to sleep and think." Indeed, he looked as tired as death. "I fear that in my exhaustion and grief I'm not seeing things right," he said more to himself than to the girls. In his mind he heard a retort from Jack Kintapush, *or maybe you're just startin' to see things right for the first time.*

James shook his head to clear his mind.

"I need you to stay below. You can't come up to the toyshop any more. The windows are broken, and you could be seen. Stay below, and I will come back for you."

"Where is Mommy?" Isabella asked, not making eye contact with James, her eyebrows furrowed.

"We took her to…" he paused, thinking of what to say. "She's in a better place," he said, and he thought a moment silently. Then he climbed the stairs and was gone.

The girls still had the problem of food. James had said nothing about when he would return, and they were hungry and had been sick from Timony's strange food the whole night.

"It's all right, girls," said Timony trying to hide the fear in her voice. "I will get you different food. Perhaps you can make me a list of things to get?"

Chloe did not understand how Timony was getting the food, but she knew the ballerina must be doing something very hard and scary, and so Chloe felt guilty. "You don't need to get us any more. We still have some left over from last night."

But Isabella couldn't stand it anymore, and blurted out, "I can't eat any more radishes, or mustard, or mold cheese! It's not that it tastes bad, which it does, but it makes my tummy hurt, and it makes me sick in the chamber pot all night," she said insistently to Chloe. "I'm so tired from not sleeping." She looked pale, and her eyes were puffy.

Looking at her feet, Timony said, "It's okay. I can do it again. If I must."

Chloe looked up at her with pity and said, "All right, let's make a list so you don't have to do this again." She ripped off a nearly blank page from the back of a schoolbook they hated, and wrote, bread, cheddar cheese (or any cheese but blue cheese), eggs, tomatoes, milk.

While Chloe was writing in a slow deliberate cursive, Timony went to the sink in the kitchen, and tried her best to wash herself. When her pale white skin was as clean as she could get it, she returned to the center room, and took the list from Chloe.

"I think we need to fix your bun," Chloe said. "Sit here." Timony knelt, then, on the ground in front of Chloe, and Chloe brushed her hair back into a more tidy bun.

Timony stood and said, "Well, wish me luck. I will be back in the morning, when I've finished…dancing." And with a clear look of fear on her face, she left.

"She's dancing for money?" Isabella said to Chloe after she heard the trap door shut with a snap.

"Yes. Well, maybe," said Chloe.

"She must be very happy. It's what she was made to do."

"I don't think so," said Chloe.

Then Bella remembered something, and ran out of the room. In a moment she was back, carrying something in her hands. She placed it on the ground and sat cross-legged in front of it. It was the tiny elephant they had rescued from the shop the night of the arrest. The elephant swung its trunk in an appreciative way, ran in a little circle, and came back and sat, looking up at Bella.

Bella ran her fingertips down the elephant's segmented metal back, as if to pet it, and said, "Good puppy."

"Bella! Did you take that from the shop?" Chloe scolded.

"I rescued it!" said Bella defensively, and Chloe softened a bit.

"Well, I suppose the shop's closed now, anyway," Chloe said, but as she did she was interrupted by the first sound they had heard from above in days. There were steps above, heavier and sharper than any they had heard before and, by the sound of it, several pairs of feet were walking back and forth. Their pace was rhythmical, perfectly timed like a clock ticking.

Within a few minutes the footsteps had divided in two directions, one in the direction of the workshop, and the other coming toward the trap door above the stairs.

Then a sound sent a shiver down their spines. The trap door was opening! It opened further and they could hear a mechanical whirring, and a chunk, chunk coming down the stairs.

They flicked off the lights, but a second later a soft red spotlight clicked on, coming from the stairwell and sweeping rhythmically back and forth.

Around the corner from the stairs came a tall, spindly mechanical figure, with three glowing red eyes darting back and forth. It locked onto Bella, and as she ran from the room, the beam of red light stayed perfectly locked on her.

Bella ran into Mother's room, and slid under the bed, but as she did, the figure was immediately at the door. One long narrow arm, shining in the darkness, grabbed the bed and lifted it off of Bella.

Bella screamed, and crawled to the back of the room, as the spectral figure tossed the bed against the wall.

Then Bella heard a loud clang! and the machine stumbled forward a bit. It rotated smoothly, twisting at the middle, to look behind itself. There stood Chloe, a cast iron frying pan still vibrating in her hands.

It grabbed the frying pan as fast as a bird might snatch a worm from a log, and tossed it to one side.

Chloe's eyes widened in terror, and she tried to back away, but tripped on the ragged old carpet. As she stumbled the machine snatched her at the waist, and lifted her from the ground.

It then pointed the palm of its other hand at her, and the hand flipped back on hinges, revealing a large protruding

106

hypodermic needle.

Before it could jab Chloe, it had to spin around again, but as it did Bella thrust a broom between its legs and threw herself against the end of it. The metal skeleton twisted, and staggered a few steps, but in a blink the machine snapped its hand back in place, without dropping Chloe, and snatched Bella from the ground as well.

Its grip was cold as ice, and cruelly tight. It ignored their kicking and crying as it strode towards the stairwell, a girl in each hand.

As it climbed the first step, red eyes scanning the steps to make sure of its footing, Chloe looked up the stairs. She was expecting to see light from the shop above, or at least the glowing crack of light that showed the hatch was closed, but there was nothing. Something was blocking the top of the stairs.

Then, from the darkness, a massive brass hand thrust out, and grabbed the head of the specter that held the girls. The hand and head shook a moment, and then the specter's head popped like a crushed tomato. In the sparking light of the intruder's crushed skull, the girls could see the kind face of Gyrod, and his massive chest and arms. He had heard the girls fight, and had been coming down the stairs to help when he saw the skeleton carrying them up.

Gyrod scooped them to his bulky body, and treading heavily on the prone body of the spectral intruder, he carried them back into the apartment.

"I watched them searching the toyshop from across the street," Gyrod said in even tones, as Bella switched the lights on. "When I saw this one discover the trap door, I crossed the street and crushed the other. These are easy to crush. They look cruel, but I do not think they were made to fight with anything larger than a man," he said. His voice now sounded like he might be smiling, had his face been as elegantly made as Timony's.

"Father was right. It does feel good to do what you were made to do," he said. "I crushed them, to protect you."

He went on. "I followed that one," he nodded to the body on the floor, "and shut the trap door behind me. Before I could get to you, he had caught you, so I waited in the darkness of the stairs."

"Oh, thank you so much, Gyrod!" the girls both exclaimed.

"But this is not good, I fear," he continued. "I am a foolish machine. Those two will be missed. More will be sent looking for them. I'm not sure how long, but they will eventually send more, and we will be discovered."

"Can't you just crush them, like you crushed that one?"

"Yes, if they are all that come. But eventually someone will figure out what is happening, and then send something bigger."

This made poor little Bella shiver.

"There is something bigger than you?"

"Yes."

They sat silent a moment.

"What can we do?" asked Bella.

"I don't know. I will talk to James. I hope he comes back before they send more."

IAN

James stood in a dark corridor, about fifteen feet away from an office door marked "Records." His back was against the wall, and he was trying to look like he was casually reading some files from his office, but he didn't know how convincing the look was, considering the lighting in the hall was too low to read by.

After about five minutes, the door opened, and a very tired- looking guard trudged out of it. The guard walked past him, not making eye contact, for fear it would mean staying at work another minute.

As soon as the guard had left the hall, James slipped through the office door. The walls were lined with file cabinets, and in the center of the room was a large, beige metal desk with a tired old man sitting at it.

"Morning, Ortie," James said to the man, with a smile.

The man ran his hands over his bald head, and through his uneven white beard, and rubbed his eyes. "Oh, good morning," he said, trying to remember James' name.

Behind Ortie was a steel door, and on the door were the words "Proscribed Records" stenciled in black paint. The paint was so old it was peeling.

There was a spot next to the door where the paint on the wall (also beige) had been rubbed away at about the spot a man's shoulders would hit it, if he stood leaning against it.

James nodded to this spot. "You're all alone this morning. Where's your friend?"

"Oh, Charlie Baker? He's always late. He's a nice enough

guy, but I'll be damned if he's ever on time. I let the night guards go, though, no point keeping them up waiting."

Evaluating staff at the Tower was part of James' job. He had files on everybody, including Charlie Baker. James expected Charlie to be late. That's why he chose this time to come and try to talk the records librarian into letting him see some of the files on the world outside the City.

This might seem a dangerous and pointless thing, to you reading this book, but remember that James did not fully believe there was anything outside the Wall. He did not believe the government of the City was intentionally keeping secrets from the people. Even if they were, it must be for the safety of the people, he thought. Intellectually, he believed these things, as it was his job to, yet somewhere in the back of his mind a small voice whispered, perhaps go when there is no guard.

"What can I do you for?" asked Ortie. "You lose a copy on someone?"

James occasionally came down here to get a copy of a file from one of his cases, but those files were all in this office, and easily available. They were not the files kept behind the guarded door.

"No, Ortie, not today. I got a special assignment from legal, and I need to get a couple Proscribed Files."

Ortie's mouth went tight, and his brow furrowed. He sat up in his chair, and spread his hands on his desk. "Protocol is you've got to be accompanied by a C5, and at least one guard." Ortie said, all the friendliness gone from his face. "Legal should have told you that. They can't just send you down here like this." He paused. "They never get that wrong."

"I know," James lied, "but it's late, and I didn't want to bother anyone."

Ortie looked shrewdly at James. He could see James was lying, and James knew it.

"Look, we don't know each other well, so I'm gonna tell you something about me," Ortie said in a cold and threatening voice. "I'm not a damn fool, and I take my job seriously. Why do you think I work three shifts a day? For my health?" His bloodshot eyes showed that he was offended.

"No, no, no! L-Look, I didn't mean anything by it!" James said, backing up, as Ortie rose. "It was just a big mistake. I'll go."

"Yes, I think that's best," said Ortie, and he pointed at the door.

James darted out of the office in a panic. Damn, I messed that up! He thought to himself as he fled down the hall. I'm out of my element!

As soon as James had left the office, Ortie walked to a spot on the wall where a large red button had been mounted. He pressed the button with his fist, and a red light came on.

An hour later, James was slumped forward at his office desk, his head in his hands. His dark brown hair was frazzled, and his eyes stung from being up all night, and his elbows were sore from holding his head on his desk. He reached past his heavy steel hole-punch, and grabbed his tin coffee mug. He tried to drink the last swallow, but it was thick and cold and bitter.

Suddenly the door of his office swung open, and clanged violently against the file cabinet next to it. James looked up, and saw Ian's red hair and pompous face.

There was an extra bit of intensity about Ian today, as he said accusatorially, "Proscribed Records, James?"

"I have a case I'm...."

"Bullshit. James, you're cracking. Only a fool would try to talk his way past old man Rodin, and try to get into Proscribed Records." He glared at James. "You know what we do to cracked people here."

"Ian, I'm really not in the mood for your–"

"I don't care what you're in the mood for, James. I'm not here as your friend, I'm here to do my job." Ian pulled a pair of handcuffs from his belt.

"Wha–, what?" James stood up. "Aw, don't play with me, Ian. You know you're never funny when you..."

But they both knew that Ian was not playing this time.

"We got an alarm from Proscribed Records, and when the order came up, it had your name on it, James." Ian was walking around to James' side of the desk, while James was backing away.

"And you asked to handle it yourself? That's nice, Ian."

"Ya know, I've taken a lot of shit from you and your sister. I'm tired of your snobby bullshit, and I'm tired of covering up for you two while she rejects me." Ian unclasped the cuffs.

"No, Ian, you don't understand," James said, his hands out in front of him. "Audrey's dead, Ian. That's why I was going to Proscribed Records. Audrey died of the cough two nights ago."

Ian stopped in his tracks for a moment. His face froze, and James mistook it for sympathy.

"Look, you got to cover for me," James implored. "I'm all the girls have left. I've got to take care of them!"

Ian stared at the floor, but then looked up again. His face was now anything but sympathetic. "You mean, I waited all this time, and covered her ass all this time, for nothing?" He said this angrily, and smashed a fist into a file cabinet. It rang loudly.

"Hold–, keep it down, Ian!" said James, his eyes darting toward the door. "Someone will hear…"

"God DAMMIT, James! I've wasted years on that bitch!" Ian kicked James' office chair out of the way. "And she goes and dies? I got nothing from that tramp!"

"Now, hold on a second Ian, that's my sister you're…"

"That whore got herself knocked up, so I get nothing. I was nicer to her than I've been to anyone! And I get nothing!? I keep her secret, then that little slut turned down my proposal." He was yelling into the air, now. "But she still asked me to keep her little secret!"

"She was dying, Ian! It wasn't about you, it was about her children…."

"And so I'm lying at work, and risking my job… Hell, I'm risking prison! For what?" Ian was pacing now, and ranting. "Oh, no, we are done with this. I'm not keeping this secret any longer. I'm not going to take a fall for a dead slut that never treated me right in the first place. It's time for you and those kids to face the–"

Ian didn't finish. James had brought the large steel hole-punch down on the back of his skull. Ian collapsed forward, hitting his jaw on the desk as he fell, and there was a cracking sound. Then Ian slumped to the floor, his head hit the ground, and a little spray of blood fell from his mouth.

ANOTHER TOY IS BROKEN

Between two massive and coal-stained brick tenements, a huge awning had been constructed, which covered the whole street. The top of this awning was littered with trash thrown from tenement windows on the stories above it. The trash floated in pools that gathered in the drooping fabric.

Under this awning was the Night Market. The awning had been built under the guise of keeping the rain off shoppers in the street, but its real purpose was to keep the aerial police drones from witnessing the vast array of sins trafficked here.

For the first few blocks, the commerce was fairly standard. Some shops sold junk jewelry. Another sold books that had been approved, or censored by the City's Council of Safe Reading (with many sentences blacked out, or pages removed entirely). Another shop sold tragically old and battered clothing. The clothes sold here had been scavenged from places the shoppers' dared not guess, but they were affordable, if not entirely whole. Small wagons lined the streets, selling a cheese-like substance sold as cheese, or rubbery bread, or canned food that predated the City by fifty years. Fresh produce rarely appeared, and when it did it was auctioned off at obscene rates, and consumed by the richest of the city's inhabitants as luxuries.

This is where Timony had found herself, searching for more palatable food for the girls. There was fresh produce today, but the costs were beyond the meager earnings Timony had left over. She pushed past the more respectable crowd, and ventured to the second and third blocks in.

Here were slightly more disreputable businesses. Shops selling not-fully-functioning automatons, who stared out at the street with fearful looks on their metal faces, terrified of who would buy them, and for what nefarious purposes they'd be employed.

Timony passed shops selling medicines for conditions that the government of the City denied existed. Many citizens suffered from "the bends," as the food of the city was far from fresh. Others suffered "the black cough," caused by the coal-polluted air that remained trapped in the walled city. These shops sold illegal remedies for illegal illnesses, and not all of these medicines worked.

There was also a cure for "Freelanders' Disease" which claimed to remove from your head any thoughts about a life outside the City. It didn't work exactly as described. This pill simply contained an intoxicating herb which, if taken regularly, made the patient happy, content, and mind-numbingly stupid. Though not addictive, its "cure" lasted only as long as the buzz from the drug continued. Since its users were depressed without it, it was far more habit-forming than most addictive drugs.

In the blocks beyond, things began to get even more sinister. The lighting here was kept low, again to avoid detection. Rainwater collected and festered in the great awning, and perpetually streamed onto the muddy streets.

The air in the street was clouded with tobacco and opium from pipes, cigars, and hookahs smoked in the many open-air pubs that lined the streets. These clubs had names like "The Easy Win," "Tomfoolery," and "The Anthropophagist's Club." Dark eyes from the pubs' patrons stared out from under the brims of top hats, bowlers, or the

occasional fez. Many mumbled obscenities at the thinly clothed and delicate ballerina as she walked past. Crass but not entirely uncomplimentary. Neither mattered, however, as Timony didn't understand them in the least.

Except one. "Hey there, young girly, do you want to make some money?"

"I do," said Timony. She thought about her last job, and shivered. Then she inhaled, and said, "I cost $25."

"Oi, that seems like a bargain for real girlie like you!" said one whiskery and lean old man. He rose, and scratched the hole where his missing ear had once been. "That's what I'd expect to pay for a machine, not a pretty little piece of pink flesh like yourself."

Timony was confused. What did he mean by "real girlie?" She knew she was not the same type of person as Chloe and Bella and the Doctor, her father. Neither did she feel she was altogether the same as her brother, the brass giant. But surely they were all "real." As she pondered what this sallow man meant when he used the word "real," he stepped away from the table where his sinister friends alternated drags on a large hookah, and he grabbed her.

His hand fell on Timony's soft, silken smooth shoulder. He slid it downward, savoring the sensation, until her skin ended, and his fingers fell on a bare patch of gears and hydraulic pipes.

He gave a little shriek of surprise and repulsion. His friends laughed. "You're a...a...a fake!" he stammered, angry at being embarrassed in front of his friends. Timony was horrified, and confused at the same time. She hated the way he touched her, but had allowed it because she knew she would eventually be paid by him. But his talk of "fake" made her at once angry and scared.

From the shadows of a nearby alley, a large man in a long leather coat had been silently watching all this, as he watched all the girls working on this block. His job was to keep an eye on the girls, protect them if they were ever in danger, or threaten and beat them if they tried to leave. For this service he took fifty percent of what the girls were paid. When he saw Timony enter in the nearly dark streets, his first thoughts had been, "This girl needs my services…whether she wants them or not." When he saw the interaction with the skinny man, he slipped silently behind her.

The skinny man was yelling now. "You can't just go around selling yourself as a real girl!" He spat at her. "It's disgusting, and it's illegal!" His friends were drunk and laughing at him, and to try to save his dignity, he raised a hand to strike her. Timony stepped backward in fear. "You mechanical whor–" he began, but he was cut off.

The large man in the coat grabbed the skinny man's fist, and at the same time he reached up behind Timony's head, and placed his ring at the based of her neck. The "jewel" in this ring had been passed down from another time, and in it was a tiny but powerful magnet. The magnet attracted a small lever just inside the back of her skull. This lever connected her thoughts with her physical control, and with it pulled back by the magnet, her body went limp. The ring was designed to do this, as this was the man's profession.

He caught her, and picked her up, saying, "I'm so sorry, my good man. She didn't mean to deceive you. Just to sustain the dream, so to speak. Didn't want to spoil your pleasure. But if it's not your cup of tea, we'll be on our way."

At this, the man in the coat quickly carried Timony off into his alley, and the skinny man watched her limp form disappear around the corner with some regret.

JAMES' PLAN

Timony did not return that day. Nor the next. The girls finished off the last of the meal bars, and were still hungry.

"What now?" Chloe asked Gyrod.

"I don't know," he said solemnly. "I'm not made for planning."

"Can you get us more food?" asked Bella.

"I don't think so. I don't know where to get money."

"Could you just take some?"

"I could, but I think I would get caught. I saw a grocer last night, but he was always watching, and there were police as well, and a long line of people. "

"And anyway," said Bella. "You'd not be very good at blending in with people. You're big."

Gyrod adjusted himself nervously, his head bent to keep from hitting the ceiling. He looked sorry for his size.

"I am," he said slowly. "I also fear that if I left, more machines might come. I am better at crushing them, than I am at getting food."

"Well, that's certainly helpful!" said Chloe, trying to cheer Gyrod up.

There were footsteps then, above them.

"James!" said the girls, both at once. They had heard their uncle's steps so often they knew them by heart, and they ran to the bottom of the stairs.

The trap door flew open, and down came James in a whirlwind. He was not in a happy mood, and had an even more crazed look than when he had left.

"Girls, girls, girls," He said rapidly, and got down on one knee to talk to them. "We've got to leave! They will come for you soon, and we've got to get you out of here."

"Now?" asked Chloe.

"Not now, but, but, but…soon. I've got some things to do…to make…first. I– I'm not sure how, but I've got to try." And he stared into the air for a moment, his eyes darting back and forth. "Yes. Yes! I think it could work. I think they used to do this, a long time ago. It shouldn't be too hard."

Gyrod was unaccustomed to questioning humans, but he had seen broken automatons before act in a similar way, and he was concerned. "James, are you functioning…um, feeling well?"

James ignored the question. "Girls, I'll be upstairs in the workshop all night. Gyrod, I'll need your help again in the morning. Then tomorrow night I will come back for the girls, and we will leave."

James glanced around the apartment, then added, "I'm afraid you won't be able to bring anything with you."

"That's okay," said Bella. "We don't have anything, anyway."

James hugged the girls, his blue eyes tearful and worried. He gave them another brown paper bag, which the girls tore into immediately. As they did, James went up to the workshop.

All evening, until the girls fell asleep, they could hear James in the shop, his feet pacing back and forth, things being dropped, and loud swear words coming through the floor, each curse repeated three times in rapid succession. It was nothing like the gentle, calm footsteps of the toymaker.

When Chloe woke in the morning, she stumbled into the center room, and found James talking to Gyrod. He had bruised knuckles and a bandage on his thumb, his face was pale, and his blue eyes were dim.

"Chloe, stay here with Bella. I will be back for you this evening, when the sun sets."

"What time is that?" Chloe asked.

James' eyes filled with tears at the question. He looked overcome with guilt and sadness. He dropped to his knees and hugged Chloe.

Chloe looked up at Gyrod, confused. Gyrod shrugged.

Then James left the apartment.

Many hours later James returned, and if possible, he looked even more distraught than when he had left. He fell to his knees once more, and his ice-blue eyes looked imploringly at the girls. "I'm going to get you out. I'm so sorry to have hidden you for so long." And by this the girls thought he meant they could leave the apartment at last, and so they wondered about the fear and sorrow in his eyes. This should be a happy time, but something told them it was not.

He led them up the stairs, to the now dark and empty toyshop where Gyrod stood silently waiting. In his arms were large bundles of silk, and long but light metal pipes. James looked up at the stooping giant, and said, "Thank you, Gyrod."

James led Gyrod and the girls out of the shop into the now-crowded street. It was rainy, and dark, and immediately the girls' excitement at being "out" ended. Hundreds of sickly-looking people walked angrily past them, occasionally pushing the girls, or bumping into them, and then cursing them for walking the wrong direction. James would then apologize, and pull the girls forward.

They did not pass unnoticed. Just as they rounded the dirty black corner of a foul-smelling tenement, James looked back and saw a police officer had been watching the unusual group. The officer started towards them, but he was some way off, and James hurried the girls and Gyrod into another alley where they waited until he was sure that no one was following.

As they walked, block after block, farther than the two little girls could remember walking before, the crowd slowly thinned, until they found themselves alone next to a wall so tall the girls could not see the top of it. There was no rain now, just fog. Gyrod reached up into the dark above them, and pulled down a metal ladder. He climbed it, still holding his bundles of fabric and piping, and disappeared above them.

"Now you, Chloe," said James, but Chloe was terrified. "I've never been high before. I don't want to," she said, eyes wide.

"I'm not afraid!" said Bella, and she climbed the ladder straight away. "See, I'm a good climber! It's because of the bunk," she said, meaning her hammock bed. "I'm used to heights." And she climbed into the ceiling of fog. Chloe watched Bella turn grey, then black, then fade from view above her. She looked back at Uncle James, but he wasn't looking at her. His eyes were darting though the street, the way they had come, and this told Chloe there was no time to be afraid.

So she climbed. The ladder, though tall for Chloe, was no more then twelve feet high. At the top it was connected to a scaffolding that led to the same concrete staircase Gyrod and James had walked days before. Up they climbed, for so long that the girls' legs ached.

Finally they could climb no more. They were so tired, Bella sat down and started crying. James sat down next to her. "Let's rest. I'm sorry I'm hurrying you so, it's just that we are in a lot of danger now, and we shouldn't rest too long." He glanced fearfully back down the stairway, then up at the stairs above them disappearing into the thick fog.

"Gyrod, why don't you continue up. I'll rest with the girls, and you can get started."

Gyrod nodded slightly, and carrying his bundles climbed up into the fog.

"Uncle James?" said Chloe, when Gyrod had gone.

"Yes, Chloe?"

"Where are we going?"

Bella's head was resting on James' leg, her eyes closed. James said, "I don't really know. Out of the–" but he stopped in sudden terror as a black shadow passed over them.

126

There was a whirring sound as it passed, but whatever had caused the shadow couldn't be made out in the fog.

"Girls! We have to go on!" James leaped up in a panic, setting Bella on her feet. "Now! Run!" and he herded them up the stairs as fast as their weary legs could carry them.

At the top of the stairs, the fog ended and they found themselves on the top of the massive concrete Wall. The sky was black and filled with stars. Behind them, on the side where the stairs were, they could see a thousand buildings stabbing up out of the fog. But on the other side of the Wall was nothing. The stars ended, and there was blackness above and below.

At this view, James' heart sank. When he had pictured this moment, he had pictured a sunny day, like his last visit to the top of the Wall. He pictured smiling, awe-struck girls, looking out at the beauty of nature. And he pictured himself telling them he was taking them there. But the sinister blackness showed the girls nothing.

Perhaps twenty feet down the wall from them was Gyrod, busy with the silk and pipes. He was assembling a massive kite that James had built in Calgori's shop the night before. It was much like the kites the Doctor had sold, though many times bigger, and under it hung several leather belts with thick brass buckles. The kite was perched precariously on the wall, pointing into the darkness beyond the City.

James led the girls by the hand, running. A wind was picking up, and the sky was turning from black to grey. When they reached the kite, without asking, he picked up Bella and began strapping her onto the bottom of the kite. Chloe, now realizing his plan, screamed and stepped back in terror, nearly falling off the Wall back into the city.

James released Bella, who had not yet been secured, to grab Chloe. Bella rolled forward and would have fallen off the far side of the wall herself, if not for Gyrod's inhumanly quick hand snatching her up by the back of her overalls. He pulled her to his chest, and stared doubtfully at James.

James was horrified, and he could tell he was losing control of what was happening. In his fear he grabbed Chloe painfully tight by both wrists and shook her. "You have to be more careful!" he yelled, and Chloe's face went red, her eyes filled with tears, and she cried.

"Gyrod, strap Bella in!" he yelled.

But Gyrod remained still. "James, you've never made anything before. I'm worried that–" Gyrod began, but James gave him such a look of terror-fed anger, that Gyrod stopped.

"It's too late to have a doubt!" James screamed at Gyrod. "It's too late! We don't have a choice now!" And James turned back to Chloe, and angrily said, "It's too late, Chloe! There is nothing else to do now. We can't go back." She closed her eyes, and cried, and tried to pull free of him.

Then James took a deep breath, wiped the tears from his eyes, and exhaled. When he spoke again, he was once more the calm loving uncle she knew.

"I need you to do as I say. This seems scary, but it will work. I just need you to trust in me." And so Chloe tied herself into the second harness.

The third, larger belt dangled empty next to her.

Then a gust of wind caught the kite, and it bucked,

causing Bella to let out a little shriek. Gyrod grabbed it to hold the girls in place, but something small and metal fell from Bella's pocket. A tiny mechanical elephant rolled to the inner edge of the wall, and toppled into the fog. There was a soft "clink!" as it landed on the stairs a few yards below.

"I'll get it," Gyrod said quietly, and before James could say, "Let it go!" Gyrod swung himself off into the fog.

James desperately grabbed at the kite now. The wind was picking up, and he could barely hold it down, as he was much lighter than the brass giant.

"Girls" he strained, "I don't think we can wait. I can't hold it much longer. Are your belts tight?" The girls stared down into the blackness below them in terror, and grabbed onto the straps with all their might.

James reached for the third belt, and grabbed it just as the wind jerked the kite out of his other hand. He strained to pull the kite back down, trying to figure out how he could strap himself into the bucking kite.

And then he heard a man's voice.

"James!" The voice was filled with hatred.

James stared down the wall, and saw a figure in the darkness. It was the silhouette of a man, tall and athletic, wearing a police inspector's uniform. He held a long thin pistol. In the darkness James could barely make out the officer's red hair, but he recognized the voice.

"James!" said Ian again. "What are you doing to those children!"

"Ian?" James said in shock. "Now, now, now, you just

stay out of this, Ian!" he stammered. "This is none of your business!"

"Oh, this is exactly my business," Ian said. "You're not allowed to be here. Are those Audrey's kids? Those girls are not allowed to be here! They should be…" he paused, savoring the implications, "relocated."

"L-look, Ian, you don't have to have anything to do with this. You can just turn and go. Save yourself the guilt! Walk away."

"Guilt? What guilt!?" said Ian, his pistol raised, pointing at James. "Why am I supposed to feel guilty? For saving these children? I'm supposed to feel guilty for that? You are obviously going to kill them with this bullshit contraption you scraped together! Or should I feel guilty for arresting a man who assaulted an officer?" Ian said, tilting his head so James could see the bandage on the back of his scalp. "Or should I feel guilty for arresting the man who threw a body from the Wall several days ago?? This is my job, James, I don't feel guilty at all!"

While he was talking, James was on his knees, slowly backing into the harness under the kite. "Now Ian, I'm not trying to harm the girls. This City has no place for them, it doesn't want them. Just let me take them away." And he pulled the buckles together at his waist.

"Stop!" Ian yelled, and he cocked his gun. "Let go of that, or you'll force me to shoot!"

The wind was picking up, and the kite started bucking again. James could barely hold on, and it pulled him back out of the not-yet-fastened harness. He struggled to hold the kite, and tried again to pull it back into a place where he could fasten the belts around his waist.

"James, this is your last warning. If you don't let go of that kite, I'll be forced to shoot!" Ian thought the motion of the kite was the result of James, not something James was trying to prevent, and he held his pistol with both hands, aiming at James' leg.

"Let go of the–" Ian started to yell again, but as he did, the wind thrust the kite up, which pulled James suddenly to his feet. This sudden motion startled Ian, and the gun went off.

There was a huge flash of metal, cutting off Ian's view of James and the kite. As Ian's eyes focused he saw the hulking form of Gyrod in front of him, lunging towards him, eyes red with anger.

The pistol went off three more times. The first two bullets rang harmlessly off of Gyrod's armor. But the third bullet found a seam, and slipped deep into Gyrod's chest.

There it found a gear. A small but crucial gear that connected Gyrod's spiral spring to the cluster of other gears that supplied momentum to his arms or legs when he moved with great force. The bullet hit this gear solidly, and although the hot lead of the bullet was much softer than the cold brass of the gear, the momentum was enough to bend it ever so slightly. As Gyrod stepped forward, the bent gear lost purchase with the other drive gears, and with a "shreek-chicka-chicka-chicka!" Gyrod's whole body seized up, and he stumbled, eyes blue with terror, and fell from the Wall into the blackness beyond the city.

Ian watched him fall, now in shock at the sight, and dropped his gun. Then he looked back toward the kite.

James was on his knees, holding onto the belts with both hands, the kite dangling over the ledge. Around James' legs, blood pooled. A bullet hole in his leg was gushing. His eyes were going dim, and his hands were slowly opening. Letting go.

The girls were screaming.

"Ian, help me…" he said. Then swooning, he let go. Ian leapt for him in sudden tears and desperation, but it was too late.

James fell from the Wall into the darkness.

DO SMALL GIRLS BLEED IN HEAVEN?

A wind pushed at the kite the girls were strapped to, and it pulled them to the edge of the wall. The kite teetered precariously for a moment, before slipping off and leaving Ian grasping in air, trying to stop them from falling.

The kite spun, and twisted as it fell, hitting the Wall, and dragging the girls down it. It cut their faces, hands, and knees, and knocked tiny Isabella unconscious.

Then a gust of wind grabbed it, and the nose swung upward. The kite began to glide along the side of the Wall, dragging one wing.

Then another gust came up the wall, and lifted Chloe and the unconscious Isabella high up, passing the top of the Wall. The City was now visible, but something else was visible too. The sun was beginning to rise, the sky turning a dark pink, and Chloe could see the tops of trees. On this gust of wind, as if some gentle hand was guiding it like a toy airplane, the kite slowly turned towards the forest, and gently soared away from the City.

Chloe was badly hurt, but she hardly noticed. She could see birds. Not the grey and black and filthy birds of the City, but brightly colored flocks of tropical birds, swarming in a tree far below. The birds were singing with the joy of the dawn.

Far to the South, Chloe could see the sparkling blue waters of a Caribbean sea, as the sun climbed swiftly into the sky.

She looked back towards the City, still in shadow. The sun rising behind it was unable to pierce the ever-present fog held in the city's walls. The City looked sinister and foul, as if it was a filthy monster angrily watching her leave. So, with a shudder, she turned to look forward again.

Now between the trees she could see the heads of long-necked beasts. They stood several stories tall, gently feeding on the lush leaves around them. One slowly watched her fly by.

Then Chloe heard a small, weak voice.

"Have we died?" asked Isabella, wiping blood from her eyes and looking at the beautiful forest below.

"Maybe," said Chloe. "But I don't think so. I don't think we'd hurt so much if we were dead."

"And anyways," Bella added, "I don't think anybody bleeds in heaven."

The girls drifted softly for what seemed like hours, not descending much at first, as gusts of wind kept grabbing them and throwing them back skyward.

Eventually they did descend, and as fate would have it, the kite dropped into a field of wild sugarcane, the metal pipes on the front of the kite absorbing much of the collision. The girls dangled a few feet from the ground, and hung there, wondering what to do.

"Should we unbuckle?" Chloe asked Bella.

"Nothing else to do," Bella answered, and with a small struggle, she unfastened her belt and dropped to the ground.

Chloe did the same, and soon she was on all fours next to Bella, hands and feet in the tangled grass between the shafts of sugarcane.

They stood up, and stepped out from under the giant kite.

"What do we do?"

"I don't know. Doesn't the air smell sweet? It smells like clean soft food in your mouth."

"Or like clean water."

"No, I know! It smells like the wind from the rooftop Gyrod took us to!"

"Better, I think."

Then Bella was silent, as she thought of Gyrod falling from the Wall. "Can automatons die?" she asked.

"They can break, I know that." Chloe said solemnly. "Timony was afraid of breaking."

"Hey!" said Bella, "What's this?" She was pulling at a leather bag they had not seen before. It had been tied just behind them on the kite. Bella pulled it loose, and it fell heavily to the ground, where it lay in the sweet smelling grass.

The girls opened it slowly, eyes wide, like you'd picture pirates opening a newly discovered treasure chest. Inside were three very large bricks of cheese, a thick dried sausage about a foot long, a loaf of hard bread, a lighter, and a box of bandages.

Bella snatched the bandages immediately, and said, "Let's take turns being doctor," in the matter-of-fact voice of a child declaring that a game has begun.

Bella happily applied bandage after bandage to Chloe's

many cuts, all while inventing a story of a doctor in an office attending to a patient who had fallen down the stairs because she fell asleep while listening to the sounds of a toyshop above her. Bella had not had many experiences to draw from.

When she was done, it was Chloe's turn to be doctor but Chloe became worried. The gash in Bella's head was much bigger than any of the bandages in the box.

So Chloe took off her sweater, and took off the shirt she wore under it. Then she put the sweater back on (which was now itchy) and tied the shirt tightly around Bella's head. A small red spot appeared on the dirty white shirt, and began to grow.

"We should walk. See if we can find someone to help," she said in worried tones.

But Bella, being made of the infinitely indestructible stuff a kid is made out of when there are more fun things at hand than crying, stood up and said, "Let's play jungle explorer!" She pushed forward into the sugarcane field, making swishing chopping motions with her hand.

Chloe grabbed the leather bag, and followed.

A Wagon Train, and Indians

After many pretend jungle adventures, the girls eventually came to a clearing by a river. Downstream the river plunged into a dark forest of large trees and shadows that moved like huge beasts, which scared the girls. Upstream, to their right, the river was surrounded by a grassy field. Having no other direction to go, they headed towards the field.

Flowers grew in the field. Thousands of bright orange poppies, so colorful they practically glowed in the noonday sun. These were the first flowers the girls had ever seen, outside of picture books, and they were mesmerized and enchanted.

They picked a hundred each, carrying them in their upturned blouses, and dumped them into a big pile. Then they pushed the pile into a big circle, and played "baby bird," curling up in the center of the circle.

They ate cheese and bread from their bag till their tummies were full. A warm wind blew over them, fragrant and clean, and the sun soaked into their skin, and fed their souls in a way nobody in the City had ever felt. Birds circled overhead, and white puffy clouds drifted by, and it felt like a dream. Better than any dream either of them would have known to have.

They slept in the sun for hours, being healed and nourished by it. The sunshine soaked into their skin, and into their chests, and even warmed the spots between their toes, which had never been warm before.

When Chloe woke, her eyes were still shut against the bright sun. Something was on her hand, soft but heavy. It felt...fuzzy! She opened her eyes, and saw a bunny was sitting on her hand, nibbling at the bread sticking out of the leather bag.

She startled, and sat up, and the bunny darted a few yards away, and watched her.

"Bella, wake up!" she said, and Bella rolled over and rubbed her eyes.

"What's wrong?" Bella asked.

"Nothing. We've got a friend."

Bella opened her eyes, and looked around until she saw the rabbit. "OOOoooOo!" she exclaimed.

But past the bunny she saw the most colorful thing she had ever seen. A house on wheels, three stories tall, with brightly colored woodwork, and stained glass windows. Lanterns of brass and colored glass hung from it, as did ropes of colored flags, laundry, bushels of drying herbs, drying fish, sacks of sundries, and barrels of water or wine.

There was a bright red door in the side of the wagon, with stairs that could be lowered when not in motion. Above the door was a hand-carved gold sign that read The Far Wanderer.

This giant vardo was attached to an ancient machine, the cab of which had been, in another century, the front a five hundred horsepower semi-truck. It wore a wreath of spare tires and gas cans, and its windows had been completely broken and gone for at least sixty years.

The back of the three-story gypsy wagon was attached to a flat trailer. The trailer had been filled with cultivated soil, and planted with fruits and vegetables, and at the very end of the garden was a small chicken coop,. Six chickens wandered the garden, clucking happily while removing bugs from the plants (and fertilizing the crops).

Standing up in awe, Bella looked around and saw three similar house-vehicles, each with its own sign over the door. The Vagabond House, which had two double-story houses, complete with roof top garden and giant water tank (made of an old septic tank), pulled behind a rusting yellow school bus, sat down the field from the Far Wanderer.

As Bella watched, four little girls, two boys, and a pack of huge dogs jumped out of the bus, the girls doing somersaults and cartwheels, and the boys throwing a blue disk back and forth while the dogs leapt in the air trying to catch it.

An adult man stepped from the driver's seat, rubbing his rump, as a plump and rosy-cheeked mother waddled out with a picnic basket and gourds of cold tea.

To Chloe, the skin of the family seemed unusually brown. This was not as much due to ethnicity as to exposure to a healthy, unfiltered sun in a way Chloe had never seen before. The people of the City, had they been there, would have told Chloe this was unhealthy. They would make up medical terms and diseases with no symptoms other than coloration.

To Chloe's eyes, having heard only of brown-skinned people in old books, she thought these looked like "Indians." They were, in fact, a mix of a hundred ethnicities, as were the people of the City, but their different lifestyle made them look completely foreign. Many infinite combinations of features and colors had blended, and then sun-tanned over hundreds of years to the point where race was no longer important, if it ever had been.

Chloe's natural inclination at seeing these people was to hide. This had been her whole life, and she knew nothing else. "Hide so you are not seen." But she was in the center of a field, and there was no place to hide. Just as she was wondering if she should grab Bella's hand and run, she noticed Bella was no longer at her side.

Looking around in a panic, she saw Bella had run all the way up to the children, and was now chatting cheerfully with them, and joining in their somersaults. Chloe had a brief moment of panic. Then she exhaled, and slowly approached.

"I'm Katina, this is Ashi, Jessy, and Suki, and that's Jaxom and Trout," said a little braid-headed girl cheerfully, as Chloe walked up. "Where is your tribe?" she asked, looking behind Chloe and Bella.

"Tribe?"

"Yeah, where's your family? Where's your train parked?" asked the boy called Trout, a little accusatorially.

"It's just us," Chloe said shamefacedly, and all the children became hushed. This was not the first time they had come across children in the plains, wandering alone.

"Io, that's like Jaxom," said Trout.

"Yeah, mum and da were eaten," said Jaxom. He said it as if he was bragging, but Chloe thought she could see sadness back behind his eyes.

"Suki and Ashi, too!" said Katina, not wanting the boys to get any extra points in the introduction.

"Oh, now who's this?" said the mother in sympathetic tones, walking slowly up to the group of children. She got down on one knee.

"This is Chloe and Isabella," said Ashi. "Their parents were eaten."

Chloe and Bella said nothing. That seemed like a different life, like a dark dream they had woken from, into another dream that made no sense. They knew their

141

parents had not been "eaten," but they didn't feel like talking about it, so they said nothing.

"Oh, such a pity," the mother said. "Well, come and get some lunch. I guess you'll be with us now."

The religion of the Neobedouin has no deities, but they believe that the world is ambivalent and self-serving, and it's up to humans to bring justice to the world.

Courage brings you freedom, and strength brings you comfort and security. Lack of courage and strength takes away freedom and comfort. Friends and family bring strength and intelligence, and kindness brings friends and family. A circle of strengths, each feeding the other. Courage, Strength, Kindness, and family.

So each night before bed they pray,

"May I have the courage to remain free,

The freedom to be strong,

The strength to remain secure,

The security to remain kind,

The kindness to remain loved,

The love to remain courageous."

~Neobedouin Prayer

Because of these beliefs, they would never hesitate to take in two lost little girls. People in the City would be afraid of the financial commitment, since they all lived on fixed incomes and had fixed expenses set to exactly their incomes. But the free peoples of the wasteland don't have incomes. They have the fruit of their labors, and more hands will produce more rewards. So in the end, a growing tribe has an easier job of things.

The girls ate, and played all day with the kids and the dogs. At sunset large fires were built, and a hand-cranked record player was brought forth, and it played quiet but cheerful trumpet music from an age before memory. The kids danced and played in the grass by firelight, and were as happy as they could remember.

As the firelight dwindled, they heard a rumble growing in the distance. It grew until it was the only thing they could hear, and then, into the circle of light cast by the fire, a motorcycle emerged. It was black but dusty, with rusted chrome, a wide rear tire, and a large and narrow front tire. On it sat a man, hair and massive beard as white as snow, skin of tanned leather, and eyes sparkling blue. In one fluid motion he dropped his kickstand, swung his right leg from the bike, and walked towards the adults who sat in folding chairs drinking wine from gourds.

In a hushed voice, he said, "We shouldn't stay tonight. We don't need to leave this instant, but we should be driving by dawn."

He paused to remove a writhing bug from his soft beard.

"What are we talking about?" asked the man who had carried the gramophone from the Vagabond House.

"Hyaenos," he grumbled, and the other adults sat up.

A mother stood, then, and clapped her hands to get the kids' attention. With a huge smile, and cheer in her voice, she said, "Okay, kids, bed time! Ashy, wake Jaxom. Come on everybody, bed-bed!"

The kids were shepherded towards the caravans, and Chloe and Bella found the uppermost floor of the Far Wanderer was the children's floor. Walls were lined with triple-story bunk beds covered in hand-woven blankets and handmade toys. Lanterns hung from decorative ropes, and illuminated countless drawings made by the children. The drawings all depicted happy children playing in sunny fields, with wheeled houses in the distance.

The dogs lay here, too, at the top of the stairs, noses downward, ears erect, focusing on the kids or the noises outside. Chloe fell asleep, watching the dogs' ears flick this way and that, focusing on a dozen things she could not see.

A NIGHTMARE

Isabella's head hurt, and the pain was keeping her on the edge of sleep, not letting her go fully in or come completely out.

She must have been asleep for a while, because she couldn't remember where she was. She hazily peeked out from under the blankets, and saw a room she couldn't remember. The walls were painted wood, and everything in the room was shaking. Extinguished lanterns swung from the ceiling, toys rolled about on wooden floors she didn't recognize. It was loud, terrifying, and she could make no sense of it.

She leaned out of her bunk to look down at Chloe, and saw her sister sleeping below her. She started to climb out, but the shaking of the room knocked her off the bed and onto the floor, which was much further away than she was used to.

She heard voices. Men were yelling to each other outside the room. She noticed a window, which of course her apartment under the stairs did not have, and she stared at it, puzzled.

Outside the window, she saw the chest of a man scuttling by. He had a beard, and wore a paisley vest, with a brass revolver drawn in one hand. He seemed to be clinging to the other side of the wall like a spider.

Then she heard several loud cracks, accompanied by bright flashes outside the window, and followed by the screams of some beast she had never heard before.

This is a nightmare, Isabella thought. I need to find Mommy.

In her dreams, Mommy was not sick, but a strong protector. Bella would search for Mommy in the apartment, while creatures chased her, but in the dreams the apartment had infinite rooms and the nightmares would not end until Bella found the room Mommy was in. Mommy would then protect her from the creatures.

So Bella looked around the children's bedroom, and saw the only exit was a staircase leading down. She ran to it, falling against the walls and tripping on toys, then stumbled down the stairs.

On the next floor she found larger beds, four in total, but Mommy was not in any of them. The beds were all empty.

Then Bella heard the terrified voice of a young girl calling her name. Is that my own voice? Bella wondered.

Through the shaking walls, she could hear the howls of monsters, so she ran to the far side of the room and down the next set of stairs.

Now she was in a kitchen she didn't recognize, with hanging pots and pans swinging and clattering. A table and chairs were attached to one wall, and in the other wall was a door. Bella ran to it, and fought with the handle. Above her, and outside, she heard more loud cracks, then a man screamed in pain.

The terrified little girl yanked at the door handles, and the door swung open. The wind blew in and threw her hair into a wild dance. She saw stars, and trees flashing by in the dark, and suddenly the floor bucked hard.

Bella lost her balance and fell from the caravan into the night.

Chloe woke because Bella had stepped on her leg. She had often woken this way, but this was different because now the room was moving.

Chloe remembered having trouble falling asleep. Bella had crawled into the bunk above her, and was instantly snoring loudly, but Chloe sat quietly in the strange bed listening to the other kids chatter about their day. It reminded her of listening under the stairs to the kids in the toyshop, and for some reason that soothed her in the strange bedroom. By the time she had fallen asleep, the house was already in motion.

But now she was awake, and she watched Bella stumbling about the room in horror. She tried to tell Bella what was going on, but the sleepwalking child couldn't hear her sister over the sounds of motion.

Then Chloe heard the shots, and saw the flashes out the window, and she saw Bella run from the room in fear.

So Chloe stumbled out of her bed to the ground. She was not used to being in a bunk, and she hit the ground hard. She scrambled to her feet, and pushed herself towards the stairs, calling "Bella! Bella!" as she watched her sister stumble away.

When Chloe arrived at the next floor, Isabella was just disappearing down the stairs on the far side of the room. Chloe ran after her, but the swinging floor knocked her into the footboard of a bed. She crawled over it, and stumbled down the next flight of stairs.

On this floor she saw her sister, frozen in front of an open door, her hair wild in the wind. Chloe froze, terrified, as the floor bucked and Bella toppled like a rag doll out of the caravan.

Chloe ran to the doorway and saw the body of her sister rolling in the dust, already far behind the house truck.

With nothing else to do, Chloe closed her eyes, and jumped.

Hunted

Chloe tumbled, in pain, rolling and spinning, and finally came to a stop in the dust at the roadside. If an adult had taken that fall, they would have broken several bones. Chloe was cut and hurt, but that was all. Nevertheless, she hurt a lot, and having nothing else to do, she let herself cry. Her tears stuck in the dust on her freckled cheeks.

Then she felt a small arm around her shoulders.

"There, there," said Bella, knowing that's something someone says to console a hurt person, and not knowing what else to say. Then, "Where are we?" she asked, looking around them.

"Bella! You sleepwalked right out of the house-truck!"

Bella didn't have an answer for this. She didn't exactly feel guilty; she had no idea what had happened or where they were. She didn't remember doing anything except waking up on the ground, and hearing her sister crying.

So Bella looked about in the darkness, trying to understand what was going on. Finally she said, "Well, anyway, where are we?"

"I don't know. You fell out of the house-truck, and I came to get you, but now they are gone."

"Should we follow them?"

"I guess so."

So the girls stood, and followed the tracks in the dirt, all the while being watched by glowing eyes in the darkness.

They walked for hours, the sky turning from black to dark blue, revealing the grasslands around them. Still long before dawn, they saw perhaps the strangest thing they had ever seen dart across the road ahead of them. It was roughly the size of a large dog, but with a hemisphere of segmented shell over small scampering feet.

It stopped midway across the road, and a small head pointed at them from under the shell, and sniffed. Then it ran into the bushes and out of sight.

"What the heck!" Chloe said.

You and I of course would recognize this as an armadillo, grown to immense size. To the girls it might as well have been from outer space.

"That was weird! But it seemed nice. I wish we could ride it."

"Yeah, I'm getting tired. Let's find a place to sit."

At the side of the road was a large rock, so they sat on that in silent exhaustion.

After a while Bella said, "Something is confusing my brain."

"What's that?" asked Chloe.

149

"If the house-truck is moving faster than we are walking, doesn't that mean it's actually getting further away the longer we walk?"

"Yeah, I think so," said Chloe, realizing defeat. "But what else can we do? I don't know another direction to walk. It's still too dark to see anything."

Bella stared at her feet. "I don't have shoes."

"Me either."

"My feet hurt."

"Mine too," Chloe said, and she looked worried at the bleeding soles of her shoeless feet. Then she said, "You know, adventure doesn't feel like adventure when it's happening to you. It just feels like it sucks."

Cicadas sang around them in the moonlight. The stars sparkled overhead, and somewhere in the distance they heard a wolf howl. The sound was immediately followed by another, much closer and more aggressive sound; a moaning, warbling animal sound.

Then a beast the size of a large dog strode out of the bushes across the road. It had bristly, dirty fur, spots like a leopard, wicked eyes and a toothy grin. The fur around its mouth was stained red. It walked towards the girls, head down and bobbing, but never breaking eye contact.

Another appeared in the bushes to its right, and then another to its left, and yet another appeared in the bushes behind the girls. The beasts yipped and warbled at each other, and sniffed towards the girls.

The beasts didn't walk directly towards them, but around them, in an ever-narrowing circle, sniffing at their bloody feet and hands. If either girl would break eye contact with a beast it would jump closer to the girls with a "yip yip yoop!"

Bella took Chloe's hand, and the two stood back to back, shaking with fear. They huddled together, until of one the beasts grabbed Chloe's blouse and tugged, which spun her away from Bella, and down to her hands and knees. Bella kicked at this one, and it backed away, but another tugged at the back of Bella's overalls, and she fell down. Chloe stood again, but the shoulder of another circling beast hit her, and she fell again. When she tried to stand a third time, striking out with her hands, and yelling angrily, her leg was pulled and she slid out onto her face.

Then all the animals lunged in, one sinking its teeth into Bella's ankle, another pulling at her arms, another dragging Chloe by the back of her hair. Bella screamed in pain and terror, which made one of the creatures snap at her face, growling. It was as if these creatures were trying to enforce their own rules. You will lie down now and quietly die.

One of the beasts sat on Bella, pinning her while another licked the blood from her feet. But suddenly the sitting monster flew sideways into the air. Two more creatures were lifted ten feet above the girls, their necks snapped, and their bodies cast aside.

Bella looked up and saw above her two angry red eyes.

"It's me," Gyrod said. "I'm sorry it took me so long to catch up."

He kicked out at the remaining beasts, propelling one into the bushes ten feet away. One of them jumped and bit at his leg, but upon receiving a mouth full of brass and steel it howled in pain. Then it barked at the injustice of it all, and disappeared into the bushes.

Gyrod bent slowly and picked both girls up in his arms, and the girls cried and hugged him.

SCAVENGERS

Gyrod strode down the road until dawn, holding a girl in each arm, until the sun had turned the sky a light pink, and birds were singing in the bushes around them.

The girls were too tired to go on, as they could not sleep in the metal man's arms. So he laid them in deep grass, and sat cross-legged around them, his legs a protective wall. He looked at this, and it reminded him of the City. He thought maybe he understood a bit how it had come to be.

When the girls woke, they were hungry, so he picked them up again and started walking. After an hour, he came to a hill that turned out to be the remains of a house. Its roof had mostly caved in, and vines and grass had grown over it so thoroughly that from a distance you could see nothing but the plants. He set the girls on the ground, and they watched as he lifted and pulled through the crumbling roof of the house.

Once this was done, Chloe and Bella ran to the edge of the hole Gyrod had uncovered.

"Maybe that can? No, the silver round thing," Chloe said.

Gyrod handed her a can of evaporated milk, maybe a hundred years old.

"This won't do, but look for more like this. This is a can, and there is food in them sometimes. It's not always good, but mostly."

In total they retrieved three cans of creamed corn, one can of corn beef hash, five cans of tuna fish, and a can of sardines. The girls opened the sardine can first, as it had a key they could turn to open it, but the smell was horrible, and whether this meant it was spoiled, or just disgusting, the girls could not guess.

They feasted on the tuna and corn with their fingers while Gyrod set other rescued treasures around them. A pair of small plastic sandals, a pink plastic Barbie-doll with no head, a sleeping bag still in its department store packaging, a large bowl, and a pair of rubber rain boots. Chloe put on the boots, and Bella the sandals.

Bella picked up the doll and looked around for something she could use as a head. Gyrod silently set a large plastic baby doll head in her lap, and Bella found it could awkwardly attached to the much-too-small body of the Barbie. It looked comical, but friendly, and this made Bella smile.

After lunch, Gyrod straightened out a crushed aluminum garbage can, and attached a rusty chain to it. He filled this with some of the salvaged supplies he had gathered, and slung it on his back like a backpack. He then picked the girls up, and strode off across the field, the sun now high overhead.

They walked all day, and the sun began to set, staining the world crimson, and as it did, Bella spoke to Chloe.

"None of those kids had their actual parents."

"I think Katina and Jessy had their real parents," Chloe said. "Well, I think they were all real parents. Just not the parents they were born with. They all seemed huggy and lovey."

"Yeah," said Bella with longing. "So I think in this

154

world, you have to find parents."

"Maybe," Chloe said, a bit darkly.

"Is Gyrod our parents?"

All were quiet for a time, then Gyrod said, "No. I can't be your parents. I think I'm broken, and I don't know how long I'll last. That bullet broke my..." He trailed off, not knowing how to explain it. "I would be unreliable as parents."

They walked a ways more in silence.

"Will those other families come back for us?" Bella asked.

"No," said Gyrod. "I'm afraid they have no way of knowing that you could have survived those beasts. They will think you were eaten, I'm afraid."

"Well anyway, it's good we aren't eaten," said Bella.

Slightly before it became absolutely pitch-black, when the moon was high and full, they came to another ruined home. This had been a large one, made of brick, so that much of the house was still standing, though it had been nearly swallowed by blackberry brambles.

As they walked up to it, Gyrod noticed that one of the walls had fallen, and protruding from under the bricks he saw the legs and torso of another brass man, much like himself, but now green with patina.

"Oh, can you save him?" Chloe asked in sympathetic tones.

"No, I don't think so. It's much too late for that, I'm

afraid." But Gyrod stared at the poor thing's chest a long time, and fingered the hole in his own chest where the bullet had entered.

"I think he wouldn't mind if I took something from him."

The fallen wall covered what was left of the dead machine's head, and half its chest, pinning its chest plate closed.

Gyrod looked around, and found a large steel rod. It was a demolition bar, long and solid, and he put it under the wall and pulled. But the wall just crumbled where the bar tried to lift it.

So Gyrod stood over the top of the dead thing, and bending down, put his massive hands under the bricks, and began to lift.

His metallic shoulders shook as he began to slowly tug. Dust clouded around his feet, and from his chest a worryingly loud scree-scree-scree! angrily buzzed. But the wall began to rise.

"Girls…" he said with some effort, while the wall shook in his hands. "Can you pull…"

And the girls, sensing his meaning, ran to the body, and tried to pull at its legs, to free it from the rubble.

But it was no use. The broken machine was too heavy.

"Okay," said Gyrod, sounding nearly defeated. "Please stand away." And with that, he strained again, and the wall began to move up again.

The sound in his chest was getting louder, so much that the girls had to cover their ears to keep them from hurting.

Also, Gyrod's normally bright eyes began to dim.

Then the sound peaked, with a scree-chicka-chicka-chicka and Gyrod froze in place. His eyes had gone out and were black.

The girls stood in fearful silence. The sun was now completely set, and the sky was nothing but blackness and stars and a moon. Crickets chirped, but in a way that made the girls think of cemeteries and graveyards.

There was a gurgling sound in the distance from some unseen water.

Still Gyrod did not move. The girls said nothing. This was bad. They didn't know where they were going, or what to do, it was pitch-black, they were in a strange land, and their only protector had just…stopped. They had seen so much death lately, there was simply no optimism left.

So they sat there, and stared at the frozen machine in the dying light.

KERMIT THE HERMIT

The girls continued to sit like that, in the darkness, staring at the lifeless body of their stoic guardian, for hours.

Finally, still hours before dawn, they heard another noise. A low rumbling in the distance that at first sounded like a growl, but as it grew, the girls recognized it as the sound of a motorcycle, like the one they had seen the day before.

"Maybe they've come back for us!" said Bella, jumping up and waving at the biker who they could now see rumbling down the pock- marked road in the moonlight.

Chloe stood and looked, as the bike drew nearer. At first it looked like two motorcycles close together, but as it came closer she could see it was a fat, long-bearded man riding on a motorcycle with a sidecar. In the sidecar were equipment, pots, tents, and many animal carcasses.

The biker stopped thirty feet away and stared at the waving girls. He looked at Gyrod, frozen under the weight of the wall, and he peered at the bushes around the house carefully.

Then he laughed loudly, and drove the noisy bike up to them.

"What are two delicate things like you doing out here all alone?" he asked in a sinister tone. The girls stopped waving.

"We were... Gyrod, he..." said Chloe, backing up, as the man rummaged in his sidecar and produced a large and odd thing that look like a rifle with a tangle of ropes dangling from the front.

"Oh, is that right?" said the man with mock interest. He stepped off the bike with the gun. "So what are your names?"

"I'm Chloe, and this is…."

"Oh, yeah?" said the man, again not listening. "I'm Kermit. Kermit the fucking hermit. You know why I call myself that?"

"Because you're a hermit?" asked Bella sincerely.

"Yeah, but you know why I'm a fucking hermit?" the rotund man said, adjusting his dirty overalls under his leather biker jacket. Chloe pulled Bella over towards

Gyrod's legs.

"Because people are shits. So I stay away from them. A hermit. All by myself."

"Why are people mean to you?" Bella asked with pure curiosity, and even a little sympathy. Chloe glared at her to shut up. They were now standing just in front of Gyrod's legs.

Kermit the Hermit took the cooked leg of some dead animal from his jacket pocket, and ripped a piece off with his teeth. The juices dripped down his mostly bare chest, and the juice soaked into his chest hair.

"I don't know, maybe it's my charming personality and my undeniable charisma." He hoisted his gun to his shoulder, and aimed it at the girls.

"So, see if you can guess why I stopped for you two girls, if I'm a fucking hermit?"

Though she didn't know why, Chloe immediately thought of Timony, coming home late at night, soiled and tired and horrified.

"I don't know," Chloe said, "but maybe you could just be nice? Maybe people would be nice to you then."

"Yeah?" Kermit said. "You'd fucking think. Nope, doesn't work," and he pulled the trigger.

Chloe screamed.

The gun fired a cluster of weighted pegs, attached to a net. As the pegs flew, they spread, and before the girls knew what was happening, the net had trapped them, and wrapped around Gyrod's legs.

"Dammit. I am a stupid fat man," said Kermit, angrily.

"Of course it would wrap around that damn machine's legs." And he jerked on the net, trying to pull it free.

Gyrod's lifeless body quivered, and they girls looked up at the brick wall barely suspended above them.

"God dammit!" said the hermit, as the net didn't come free. It also didn't free the girls, now tied to Gyrod's legs.

Kermit jerked the rope again, this time harder, and Gyrod's body spun a bit, and one of his motionless hands slipped loose from under the wall, and the wall began to crumble, showering bricks and dust around the girls.

"God fucking dammit!" he yelled, and with one final jerk, Gyrod's other hand slipped, and the wall fell. It nearly crushed the girls, but as they were tied to the brass man, his falling forward also pulled them out of harm's way. He crashed to the ground, the girls tied on top of him.

When he hit, his rigid body went limp, and a zeeeeeen-zeeen ziiip-zip-zip-zip sound could be heard coming from his chest. His eyes lit, and he lifted his head, and looked at the man.

"Aw, shit!" said Kermit, backing towards his bike.

Gyrod looked around for the girls, while trying to pull himself to his feet. He tried to stand, but the act of spreading his legs tightened the rope around the girls, and they screamed in pain. When he saw them tangled on his legs, Gyrod's eyes went red.

With a speed that would have made a sparrow jealous, one of his long arms shot out and grabbed the man by the back of his jacket. Kermit tried to wriggle out, but couldn't.

"Untie us!" Gyrod said with a growl.

161

"Let me go!" The hermit said.

"Not until you untie us."

Gyrod dragged the man over to the net, but didn't let go.

Kermit took a pocket knife from a holster on his belt, and cut away at the rope, all while complaining about "God damn waste of a good net."

Finally the girls and the giant were free, and Gyrod stood, holding the man above his head with one hand. He stared at the man with red eyes, and raised his other hand to strike the man, but he saw little Bella tap on his metal legs.

"No, you have to let him go. That's the deal."

So Gyrod put the hermit on the ground, and the hermit ran to his bike and started the engine.

"Yeah, that's the fucking deal," he said mockingly, and he started the engine, spat, and sped off into the night.

THE CABIN AT THE END OF THE WORLD

They walked all morning, Gyrod still carrying the rod he had found at the ruins, now walking with it as a staff. A fog set in. The ground became moist, and finally marshy, with swamp grass and trees appearing around them. Then they came to the end of the path, at the shore of a swamp, and they stopped.

Gyrod's eyes were misted with the humidity, and though he tried to wipe the moisture away, his metal hands were no use.

"What can you see?" he asked.

"I can see a house on the lake," Chloe said. "A little house, in the middle of the lake."

Bella tugged Gyrod's hand so he would bend over, and she wiped his eyes with her shirtsleeve, and said, "I'm really sleepy."

"Me too," said Chloe.

He straightened and looked out over the lake, and saw the house. It was a tiny cabin, with a long dock that connected it to the shore. This had once been a fishing cabin, and for whatever reason, it was surprisingly well preserved when compared to the ruins they had seen previously.

"Let's see if you girls can sleep in that house," Gyrod said, surveying the plains behind them for any wild hunting beasts.

They walked down the long tarred wooden dock, and came to the cabin door, which stood open. Gyrod had the girls stay still, as he stuck his head into the small cabin.

Inside were a table and chairs, a pair of beds, and one surprised raccoon, who chattered angrily at seeing Gyrod.

"This looks good," he said back to the girls, and he entered the one-room cabin, his head bowed to keep from hitting the rafters.

The girls followed him in, emitting excited little squeaks and coos.

"Oh, it's like a playhouse!"

"It's beautiful!"

"This is my bed!"

"This is mine!"

Momentarily forgetting their exhaustion, the kids hurried about the place. They righted overturned chairs and placed them around the table. They put their things on the beds. They made the beds, which surprisingly had blankets and pillows.

"Someone has lived in here recently," said Gyrod.

"Not too recently," said Chloe. "there are lots of spiderwebs everywhere. And spiders, too!" She stomped one of them out of existence. "It's going to take all day to clean them out." She paused, taking aim. "And a lot of stomping," and she brought her rain boot down on another scampering thing.

"Why don't you sleep, and I will clean them out," said Gyrod, looking at the now-slumped Bella, sitting like a discarded puppet on the edge of her bed. "I can reach them better, anyway."

So the girls climbed into their beds, and in a moment were fast asleep. Gyrod wandered about the room, swiping the cobwebs with his metal fingers, and when he was done, and the girls had still not woken, he stepped out onto the dock. He sat crosslegged, still holding the steel rod. He stared down the dock, and thought, "Here I can guard the girls. There is only one direction I have to protect."

While Gyrod had been clearing up the cobwebs, the angry raccoon had scampered out of a hole in the back of the cabin that only he knew about. It seemed to him highly unfair that this odd threesome could take his house, just because they were bigger than him.

He stood on a little outcropping of wood, and looked for a way back to the dock that connected the cabin to the shore. He could not find one. His perch was only a couple feet long, and it hung out over the water of the swamp.

He could go back into the cabin, and leave by the front door, but he did not know if automaton or human children ate raccoons. Given the circumstances, they just might, so he didn't dare go that way. He could still see Gyrod clumsily pacing about the cabin.

So he looked down at the black swamp water with dread, and jumped in. He swam as fast as his tiny feet could paddle, but it was no use. About twenty feet from the cabin, a massive black shape appeared in the water beneath him, and with a "snap!" he was gone. This, too, seemed unfair to him, but only for an instant.

FATHER

They lived there in the cabin for many weeks. The girls stayed mostly inside when Gyrod was home, and they "played house" which is roughly the same thing as living in a house, but you assume personas while you do it.

Sometimes Bella would be the mother, and Chloe would be the child, and they would cook and clean and eat. Sometimes Bella would be the child, and speak in a "childlike" voice that was simply an exaggerated version of her actual child's voice. But often they talked about what it would be like to have real parents.

"One day we will meet a kind lady, or man, who wants to be our mother or father," Bella said once, tired of the game and feeling lonely and sad.

"Do you think so?" Chloe said, no hope left, and trying to be satisfied with the happy ending of a sunny cabin of their own.

"Yes," said Bella with absolute certainty. "We almost had a family a few weeks ago. The Neobedouins. They were happy to be our parents. Most of those kids just found their parents–" she paused, "…it's just that I fell off." Then she sat quiet, and hugged an old white bear Gyrod had brought her.

Chloe looked at her feet.

Gyrod would go out during the days, and walk for miles around the house, picking through ruins for anything the girls could use. Canned food, clothing, shoes that had not yet rotted, and broken toys. That's where the bear had come from. It had fallen into the bayou a hundred and eighteen years before, and though the swamp had broken the toys' ability to glow at night, it had preserved the fur perfectly for a century. When it dried, Gyrod gave it to Bella, and Bella was in love.

Oftentimes Gyrod found himself in a fight. The many predators of the prairie wasteland often mistook him for meat, so Gyrod became quite good at wielding his demolition bar. He could then take the dead beast back to the girls, who would cheerfully cook it, and never complain about the vast variety of odd-tasting meat.

Each night Gyrod would sit cross-legged on the dock, and stare down towards the shore, thinking about the animals that had hunted the girls, or the man with the sidecar motorcycle and the net gun. "This is my road to guard," he thought to himself, "for as long as I can."

This worried him. Ever since the fight with the hermit, he knew that he could seize up at any time. The girls would then be left alone, and mostly likely killed. They were happy in the cabin, and it was easy to guard, but the waters around it were not safe. Twice before Gyrod had chased crocodiles off the dock, crocs who would have been more than happy to have a meal of two small girls. These were not normal crocs, but some prehistoric ancestor of huge proportions. Dealing with a normal-sized crocodile would have been no trouble for Gyrod, but these huge monsters were challenging.

One night, as the sun was setting, and the sky was turning purple between the trees, Gyrod heard a familiar sound. It was the rumble of a motorcycle, and as he looked down the dock he could see its three wheels, and its sidecar. The motorcycle rumbled to a stop about thirty feet from the brass guardian, and the rider, just a silhouette on the bike, sat silently contemplating the situation. Gyrod tried to see the man in the dimming light, but he couldn't make him out. Still, the bike looked familiar, and he thought of the hermit.

"Turn away, Bedouin," Gyrod called out. "Your tribe is elsewhere. My road ends here."

The figure got off the bike, and Gyrod tensed. If the man reached for his net gun, Gyrod would spring like a cat. Then from the corner of his vision, Gyrod saw something move in the water.

"Turn back, Bedouin. Your motion will bring the crocs. They

know I am not their food, so they leave me alone, but I'm sure

they can smell you already."

Gyrod could see one of the huge reptiles circling in the water, and he froze. The monsters typically ignored him if he didn't move, as motion was really the only way he gave the impression of life, and therefore meat. He had no smell.

But the man on the motorcycle got off, and started walking towards him. He was still twenty five feet away down the dock, when he yelled, "Gyrod, I'm here to speak to you. Your sister has sent me. She has left the City, and wants to see you!"

Sister? Gyrod thought. Could he mean Timony? What trick is this hermit up to? But how would he know about my sister? He could hear the girls in the cabin behind him come to the doorway to watch the man on the dock.

Bella and Chloe watched from behind an ancient screen door. Bella whispered to Chloe, "Maybe it's a parent? A father?"

But Chloe felt wrong about something. So she said, "No, Bella!"

Then two things happened at once. The giant of a crocodile that Gyrod had been watching approach the dock finally arrived, and halfway between gyrod and the biker it hoisted itself into the air with one claw on the dock. It sniffed, looking for prey.

But without noticing this, her eyes fixed on the biker, Bella said, "We'll never find a father if Gyrod chases them all away," and she burst out of the cabin, past Gyrod and down the dock.

Gyrod yelled out, the first emotion they had ever heard from him, and with a sound of both pain and fear he said, "This is not your father, Isabella, come back to the house!" He was pleading.

Bella did not see the croc on the dock. It was too big for her to see, just a black shape like a wall, blending in with the black trees on the side of the lake. But the beast saw her, and it opened its jaws in a slow motion anticipation of her arrival.

The biker leapt from his bike, and started to run towards Bella. At this Gyrod snapped into motion, but springing out of his cross-legged stance proved too much for him, and he froze, with a screee-chika-chika-chika ringing in the night.

The croc heard the sound, and swung its massive head

toward the automaton, but the weight of its huge body was too much for the dock. It splintered, knocking Bella off her feet.

The biker also tripped on the broken decking, colliding with the girl, and the two of them slid down the now angular dock towards the croc.

At this point, Gyrod pounded a fist into his chest, which made the scraping sound silent. He then leapt into the air like a jungle cat, and came down, wrecking bar first, on top of the head of the beast. This made a thudding sound, like the sound of hitting an inflatable boat with a baseball bat, and the beast thrashed angrily about, sending wooden planks spinning into the air.

Gyrod pulled the bar back, and thrust it into the beast's cheek. The bar sank two feet into the dark green flesh, and the beast pulled back from the dock in pain, swinging the

clockwork man like a rag doll.

Then to Chloe's horror, the biker stood, and picked up Bella. But he didn't leave. Instead, with Bella under one arm, he ran to where Chloe was hiding in the house.

Chloe ran to her bed to hide under it, just as he crashed through the screen door. He stood there a second, surveying the room, and she saw that he was not the hermit. He was a tall, broadly built man. Dusty from days on the road, with scruffy whiskers and tall spiky hair, and a kind, sympathetic look in his eye. He wore tall buckled leather boots, and a sleeveless leather tunic with spikes in the shoulders. With this mismatched appearance, Chloe could not tell if he looked more like a biker, a pirate…or a father. The man set Bella on a bench, and with a stern finger, said, "Stay!" Then, turning to leave the cabin, he was confronted by the massive hulking form of Gyrod, blocking the doorway.

The wearied automaton simply said, "My sister?"

Gyrod and the man talked all through the night, while the girls slept. Chloe woke first, and sat up in her bed listening. Was this a kindly man?

He seemed like it. Kind, but much stronger and more capable than their poor Uncle James. James had been weak, kind but too emotional, and he was not capable. Even if James had made it into the prairie with them, he could not have protected them in the wasteland. But this man, clad in leather and spikes, with sun-tanned skin and thick arms looked strong and convincing. His deep eyes seemed to sparkle with the confidence of a man who was always successful. And his deep gravely voice made him sound like he could tell great stories to tuck you into bed at night.

Chloe listened as Gyrod spoke of his broken gear, and saw at first pity in the biker's eyes, and then a determination to help.

Bella woke and slipped into bed with Chloe. She hugged her sister, and they listened. She, too, could see the kind-hearted determination and strength in the stranger's eyes, so she whispered to her sister, "Is this a daddy?"

Bella watched the stranger show a willingness to help their wounded giant. Only their beloved toymaker had treated automatons with such care and feeling of equality, so she made up her mind. Bella slipped out of bed, and right into the stranger's lap. She put her arms around him, and gave him a hug of a quality that only a small child can produce, and then looked up into his eyes, and asked, "Daddy?"

The man's eyes filled with tears, then a flash of concern, and finally conviction. With a tone that carried a promise Bella knew meant forever, he said,

"Sure."

The End

48794366R00097

Made in the USA
Charleston, SC
11 November 2015